Of Snow and Whiskers

Of Snow and Whiskers

by Andrea Marie Brokaw

Hedgie **HP** Press

Of Snow and Whiskers

Andrea Brokaw

copyright© Andrea Marie Brokaw 2017

Published by Hedgie Press

ISBN-10: 0-9847021-9-9

ISBN-13: 978-0-9847021-9-0

Cover art by Melody Daggerhart
Author photo by Andrea Brokaw
Hedgie Press logo by Amanda Ulevich

Also by Andrea Marie Brokaw:

Of Fur and Ice (A Werestory)

I'd Rather Not Be Dead

Pride, Prejudice, and Curling Rocks

This book is dedicated to my readers.
(AKA, YOU!)

Chapter One

The boy in the cage doesn't look threatening. If I were trying to describe him, I'd be more likely to call him "hapless" or "harmless" or maybe even "hopeless." Or maybe I'd use my native Russian and pull out "nezadachlivyy," which is more like "luck-less." His dim eyes brighten as they track the tray I carry. Add "hungry" to that list of adjectives.

"Hey." I slide the cage door open with my foot. It wasn't locked, because despite putting this guy in lockup, the powers that be are fully aware a lock wouldn't stop him if he wanted to leave. He's an all-were, someone who can turn into any creature he can imagine, from a blue whale down to a dust mite. No, if Mr. Atherton and company were worried about the prisoner escaping, they'd have kept him unconscious. "Ready for lunch?"

"Yeah. Sure." His words sound despondent.

"Something wrong?" I ask, immediately before wanting to smack myself for stupidity. Of course something's wrong! The guy spent weeks struggling in the Alaskan wilderness before ending up here in the basement of North Sky Academy while the local were-community decides his fate. They could elect to kill him, although I personally would bet on them showing leniency and exiling him to the detention center in North Pole. Not that I'd feel people were being nice to me if I were sent to North Pole; I've had nightmares about the place since I was little. "Sorry. Dumb question."

"It's alright." He scoots down the mattress he's sitting on and takes the tray from me to sit it in his lap. As soon as the food is moved, I catch a good whiff of the room. It usually smells like ammonia and coyote, since it's run by a were-coyote who is constantly disinfecting things. The usual smells comfort me, but today's scent has the opposite effect. Because it stinks in here. The prisoner needs a nice, long bath. And he should change clothes. There's a small stack of clean-looking things on the corner of his bed, but I guess he couldn't stand the idea of putting them on without cleaning himself. I'm surprised at Nurse Sakura for allowing him in here without a good wash. She can't be happy with the way he's making her sick room smell. "What's your name?" he asks.

"Rina." My hands flop at my sides, unsure what to do now that they're no longer holding anything. I'm cursed with a need for constant fidgeting. "Short for Katerina."

He grunts acknowledgment. "But it's Rina, not Kat. Interesting."

"I guess." Since I turn into a snow leopard once a month, I'd feel unbearably cliché if my name was Kat, but there's no point in telling him that since he can tell my species from my scent. Assuming he can smell me over his own reek.

"I'm Troy." He picks up his fork and rams it into the pile of mashed potatoes that sits beside a steak and some steamed carrots. Most people I know would have gone for the meat first. "Guess you knew that, though."

"Yeah." I shrug. "You're kind of big news. Are you really like Michaela and Kim? Because you smell like a snow leopard to me, and they seriously don't."

"Mike hates being called Michaela. But, yeah, I'm like them. And, yeah. I made them what they are. And, yeah, that makes me an asshole. At best." He says all this while shoveling potatoes into his mouth. "Hungry" was a huge understatement. He's ravenous enough that I wonder if anyone brought him breakfast.

"That's harsh." Simone would say something sarcastic about how bringing Michaela into the were-world was a criminally horrible thing to do, but Simone's not here. She's

2

serving a sentence of suspension for... well, for bullying the new girl.

"Is it?" Hazel eyes slide up from the plate to meet my gaze. "As I see things, I got Kim killed."

I shake my head. "No. You made her an all-were, but you didn't force her to run around murdering livestock and bringing attention to all of us. You definitely didn't make her turn into a demon and try to slaughter the wolf Pack."

"I should have stopped her."

The breath rushes from my body and I lean against the fence separating this cell from the one beside it. "I know that feeling. It sucks. My counselor says you can't control people though, not when they're strong-willed. And Kim certainly is... or was..."

"You think they killed her?"

"They haven't said. But they didn't bring her here with you, and I think that says something."

He looks back to his food and stabs a carrot. "All she did was kill some animals. How's that different from slaughtering the cow on my plate?"

My back straightens as I stare at him. My first instinct is to ask if he's kidding, but I realize he isn't. Where does he come from that endangering the entire community doesn't seem like a big deal? "Ignoring the wolf she killed? Eating beef doesn't tell the human world our kind exists."

"Our kind?" He shoves another carrot into his mouth. I wonder if his parents never taught him how to eat with his mouth closed or if he's just starved for both food and conversation. "Not my kind. There's only three of us. Maybe two." He looks up sharply. "We're an endangered species, and they may have just killed one of us for doing something wild animals do all the time."

"Endangered?" He's lecturing a snow leopard about being endangered? My wild cousins aren't exactly bountiful. "We're all endangered. And we'd be more so if the human world knew we were here."

His shrug implies disagreement, but he doesn't argue as he eats the last carrot and finally picks up his knife for the steak. "Guess there's still the wolf. But I can't believe she meant to kill him. At worst it was manslaughter, not murder."

The words "dead is dead" spring into my mind, but don't get uttered. Instead, I settle silently back against the wires behind me and watch Troy cut tiny little pieces of beef. He eats them much more delicately than he ate the vegetables. It's an odd contrast to just about everyone else I've seen eat, and as the official sick room volunteer, I've brought food to just about everyone in the school at some point or other.

"So how'd you get to be prison warden?" Troy asks between bites.

"I'm more of a student nurse, actually. This is usually a sick bay, not a jail."

His eyebrows go up into his dark brown hair. "A sick bay with cells?"

"Sometimes people are sick in animal form."

"Huh." He shakes his head and cuts more beef with a thoughtful expression. With his pale hazel eyes and dark Mediterranean features, I would be tempted to think he was cute if I wasn't put off by the whole turning-people-without-consent thing.

As I look at him, I realize I've already gotten used to his smell, enough to be able to pick out his body scent scent from the assortment of stenches clinging to him. And it is a far-from-objectionable scent. If this is how the all-were girls smell to guys, I can see why so many heads turned for Michaela and Kim.

He shifts as he moves the tray off his lap. "What do you know about this Warren guy?"

"Warren? Denali?" I shrug. It's a small school, so I know everyone in it to some degree. I also know why Troy asks about him; it's because Warren's decided Michaela is his lifemate. "He's a wolf. And a senior. And a pretty good guy. He won't hurt her."

"Unlike me, huh?"

"I..." I swallow and edge closer to the door. "I don't know."

His gaze narrows on my movement. "I'm not dangerous."

"I know," I lie, even though he can probably smell my anxiety.

"Really." He lets out a breath and leans over his knees. "I know I shouldn't have attacked them, either of them. But I wasn't trying to hurt them."

"What were you trying to do?" I ask against my better judgment.

"I don't know." The bed creaks as he bends further forward, then sits up suddenly. "No, that's a lie. I was sick of being alone."

"But why attack them without telling them what was going on?"

One slide of his mouth tries to smile, but the other side doesn't cooperate. "Didn't want them to say no. Told you I was an asshole."

After I leave Troy and return his tray to the cafeteria, I change and head into the gym for my daily run. It usually helps clear my mind and brighten my spirits, and I'm hopeful it will today.

The first mile on the treadmill passes quickly as I replay my conversation with Troy. I'm not sure what to make of him. I know he's done some really bad things, but something about him makes me want to be sympathetic. It's not like he doesn't seem sorry for what he did, and it's obvious he's been very lonely for a long time. I can relate. And how much more would I be able to relate if I was the only were, or even the only snow leopard, that I knew?

The second mile goes by while I try to talk myself out of liking Troy. Not that it matters if I like him or not since he's probably bound for North Pole. North Sky had a girl sent up there a few years back, but it was before I came here. Nicole, my older foster sister, told me all about it though, and that chick was apparently a total piece of work. I shouldn't be making friends with people like that.

Right as I start into my third mile, the door opens, and even though my back is to it I can tell that the person entering spends a few moments watching me before committing to coming in.

I glance over my shoulder and come dangerously close to making eye contact with the newcomer.

"Hey, Rina," Seth says.

Seth Dae is the only male snow leopard in my school, so it makes sense that he makes me a little nervous. It makes even more sense when you add in the fact that he's been engaged since infancy to my best friend, Simone, as part of a deal that ended a three-way Clowder war. It was the same deal that landed me with my foster family. Unlike me, however, Seth has decided to do something about being used as a political toy, and is Challenging to be free of the betrothal.

We were certain when he initiated the Challenge that he wanted to be free to date Michaela, but he hasn't dropped it as far as I know, even though she's obviously dating someone else now. I want to ask about it, but I'd have no idea how to even start, so I stay silent as I keep my feet moving.

The treadmill next to mine hums to life and Seth's footfalls match my pace. I glance over to see that he's dressed for working out and his long hair, a mixture of black and white that stretches nearly down his back, is tied at the nape of his neck. I keep my gaze moving, not wanting to be caught looking at him. I have no idea what he's doing here. I mean, he's obviously running, but he doesn't come in here often. He's generally more likely to be found sitting at the piano in the music room.

"It's weird," he says after a while. "Seeing you alone, I mean. Have we ever been alone before?"

Yes, we have. But Simone chewed me out afterwards, so I've taken pains to avoid it since then. The memory is almost enough to make me stop running on the treads and start running for the door, but I remind myself Simone isn't here and can't possibly know what I'm doing. Besides, is it still bad to be alone with her fiancé if he insists he isn't her fiancé?

"It's been a while," I say as I punch in a command to increase the incline of my run. A massive drop of sweat slides down my cheek, and I console myself that at least I can honestly tell Simone I was as unattractive as possible while being alone with her intended.

"Are you mad at me, too?" he asks. "I mean, I know Simone is. And I don't blame her. But I thought maybe you'd understand, at least a little."

I understand more than a little. I was taken from my family in Moscow when I was six and sent to live with Simone's in rural Alaska. When I graduate high school, I'll be sent back to a country I hardly remember without anyone asking my opinion on the matter. I try not to think about it much.

"Maybe I do understand," I admit. "But she's still my best friend."

"I know. I'm sorry."

I shake my head. "Don't apologize unless you mean it. And I don't think you do."

"So you are mad at me?"

My speed increases without me thinking about it. "Not exactly. I understand you don't want to marry her. She's a strong woman, hard to control. Hardly docile wife material."

"Docile?" He jumps off his treadmill and comes to stand in front of mine. His grey tank top really shows off the muscles in his arms as he crosses them over his chest. "What makes you think I want docile? She's not strong; she's mean. There's a big difference."

My teeth grind together as I shake my head.

"Maybe not to you," Seth goes on. "And not to me. But to other people."

It's getting hard to breathe, run, and talk all at the same time, but I grit out, "To Michaela, you mean."

"It's not limited to Mike, and you know it."

The horrible thing is, I do know it. She doesn't intend to be mean though. Well... okay, sometimes she does. But most of the time she's just trying to protect herself and the people she cares about. Even the mess with Michaela was because she was worried about the all-were hurting Seth. "She's not a bad person. And you know that."

"Maybe she isn't," he concedes. "But that makes it more important that I end this thing. Because if she's a good person, then she deserves better than someone who's with her solely because he's scared of her father."

I stare at him for several paces. It's not like that idea had never occurred to me, but something about it being said out loud by his voice rather than quietly by the one in my head makes it seem more plausible. It's been obvious for a long time that he wasn't happy with the engagement, but I always thought eventually he'd learn to see the real Simone and love her. She does deserve better than someone who has to be talked into loving her, though.

"Okay." I nod.

"Good," he says before getting back on his treadmill. "So we have a truce?"

"Yeah, I guess."

Truth be told, I wasn't really all that upset with him. I knew I should be, but... call me crazy, but I don't think arranging marriages before people have even developed their personalities is a reasonable thing to do in this day and age. I'd just never tell Simone that.

"But you did hurt her, Seth. A lot." I gasp for air. "She has feelings."

"I know. But I tried to talk to her about it before I did anything. She just wouldn't listen."

She never mentioned that to me, but it doesn't surprise me. Simone is very good at only noticing the things she wants to notice, and probably hadn't even allowed herself to realize what he was talking about.

The beep that lets me know I finished my third mile goes off, and the machine slows into cool-down mode.

Beside me, Seth brings his treadmill to a complete stop even though he's hardly used it. "I plan on apologizing for how I handled it when she gets back."

"Good." Although I hope he's prepared for her not to accept it.

I go over to the water cooler and refill my water bottle, the one from the Snow Leopard Trust with the pink snow leopard chasing an ibex on it. Slowly, I take a sip as I watch Seth from the corner of my eye. He gets off the treadmill, but hangs back like he's nervous.

"If you're training for the Challenge," I tell him, "I recommend running longer."

"I actually wanted to talk to you about that," he says.

"Me?" I tuck a very sweaty strand of hair behind my equally sweaty left ear. "I don't know anything about cat-form combat."

"No. But you do know about moving. About reflexes and endurance."

My head tilts to the side as I try to follow what he's saying. "So you want me to teach you human-form martial arts in the hope it will somehow translate?"

"Do you have any better ideas?"

"Why me? Why not ask Billings?" I ask, naming my martial arts coach.

Seth's amazingly blue eyes drop to the floor for a moment. "I did, actually. He said to talk to you. Seems to think you could use more experience teaching."

And I can't really argue with him. Part of qualifying for first dan is becoming a proper instructor. "You know if I help you, Simone will kill me."

He smiles like that was funny. "I won't tell her if you won't."

Chapter Two

As I shower post-workout, I wonder if I really am going to help Seth. On one hand, he's just as much a member of my Clowder as Simone is. On the other hand, Simone's my foster-sister. And she's really viscous when she's upset with someone, which she most certainly will be if she finds out. The simple solution of not telling her seems dishonest and sleazy, more of a betrayal than if I did it openly and just let her be angry with me.

As soon as I turn the water off, the sound of my shower is replaced by that of someone knocking on my door. I throw on my robe and rush to the knocking to reveal a blonde, pixie-haired vixen named Lyly. Words to describe Lyly include "gorgeous" and "confident," but to call her my friend is an overstatement. While she does hang with my little group whenever she's broken up with her current ex-boyfriend, this is the first time she's ever been to my room.

"Whoa," she says, her eyes on the walls I've completely covered in quotes from old songs and older movies. "Did you write all that?"

It's a ten-by-ten room and every inch of vertical surface is plastered with writing in various languages and alphabets. Some of the words are large and some small; all are in different colors. I shrug. "Not originally, but I copied it all onto the walls."

She makes a noncommittal noise and extends her arm to hold out a clipboard. "So, I'm here getting signatures to demand the Council keep the male all-were here instead of sending him to prison."

"North Pole's not really prison," I say, prompted by instinct more than conviction. It's not a prison, but a reformation camp. All the Elders agree about that, although none of them have ever told me what the difference is.

"Whatever. He doesn't deserve to go there. He deserves to be treated like any other were who comes from a human family."

"Does he?" I take the clipboard to stop her from continuing to wave it at me, but leave the pen where it is for now. "Come from a human family, I mean."

She nods quickly. "He was adopted, but yeah."

"How do you know that?"

With a sigh, she takes the clipboard. "When did you get so skeptical?"

"I..." I shrug, not knowing what to say. When did asking questions start annoying people so much?

"I know he's adopted," Lyly says slowly, her beautiful face taking on a somber cast. "Kim told me. She talked about him a lot."

"She really was obsessed with him, huh?"

"Apparently." She taps the clipboard with a delicately manicured nail. "Last chance."

Without conviction, I slide the pen out from under the clip. The back of my robe is becoming soaked with water, and I'd just as soon move on to another part of my life, one involving a hairdryer. "They're not likely to listen to us, you know."

"Maybe not." Her face morphs into a smile. "Won't know until we try though."

"I guess." My eyes go over the list of students who signed before me and stop on an interesting one. "Michaela signed it?"

"What?" Lyly snatches the list back and glares at it. "When did...? Ugh! Must have been when I left it out in the dining room for lunch."

I can't help but observe, "For someone who just found an unexpected ally, you sound really pissed off."

Her glower holds for a few seconds before she flicks her head up. "You know what? You're right. She may be a skank, but she's still a name. One that should impress people since she's one of his supposed victims."

I'm not sure "supposed victims" is really the right phrase, considering he obviously turned them. No one is arguing that he didn't, or even that he did it with permission. My common sense keeps me from saying anything about this, though.

"Lyly!" a bear named Elton calls down the hall as he runs toward us.

Like most of the polar bears, Elton is huge and seeing him hone in on us makes me feel like I'm in the puck in a hockey match. Lyly preens slightly, her normal response to being approached by a male.

Elton comes to a stop before us, short on breath. "The trial. It's starting in half an hour. The Pack just picked Troy up."

I grab the clipboard and add my name to the list of people asking clemency on Troy's behalf. I wasn't sure I was going to sign before I started to, but now that I have it feels like the right thing to have done.

"I'm crashing it," Lyly announces.

"Me too!" say Elton, his chest puffing out. I'd rank the odds of him actually caring to be very low, but he clearly wants Lyly to think he does.

As the clipboard transfers back to the vixen, I wonder if I should be joining in. Is there a point? It's not like anyone there is going to care that I talked to the guy for five minutes and don't think he's a monster.

Lyly wraps her hand around my arm. "You're coming too, kitten. We need as many species as we can get. Make them see this affects more than just the wolves."

"I need clothes," I say without pause before pulling my arm free and dashing into my room.

Part of me wants to slam the door shut behind me and hide under the bed, but it loses the vote to the part of me that doesn't want to see someone suffer more than he needs to. It's not my conversation with Troy that finalizes my opinion, but seeing Michaela's name on the petition. If she can forgive him, who am I not to?

I let the door close gently and throw on the first things I can grab. I'm not sure pink snow boots, jeans, and a well-worn gray sweater are really appropriate attire for a trial, but there's no time to pick out anything else. There's barely time to drag my parka from the closet and toss my crucifix around my neck. I don't wear it often, but this seems like the time to do it. I run a brush through my long, constantly tangled, blond hair before yanking a wool cap over the wet mess, and call it done. I'm going to smell like a drowned sheep for the duration, but people can deal.

Lyly emerges from her room as I pass the door and flashes me a smile of solidarity.

The wolves use a bar in town for their meetings, so Lyly and I cram into her SUV with Elton and a couple other bears. Elton calls shotgun and leaves me sandwiched in the backseat between two people I barely know, Charles and Francis. Being around polar bears always makes me feel like a ghost. Their Inuit-like skin is many shades darker than mine, but the main issue is just that they seem so full of life, even when they're just sitting still.

Since Lyly is seventeen, it's not actually legal for her to be carting around so many non-relatives, but that's one of the human laws that we weres pretty much ignore. And it's not really enforced in our county, where most of the police force is furry.

When we get to the bar, Denali's, we find it nearing the plus side of max capacity, but we manage to squeeze in just before they stop admitting new people. There are still ten minutes before the trial is supposed to start, and I imagine a lot of people are going to be turned away.

Time crawls by as I shuffle anxiously in the tiny space allotted to me. It's too warm in here, and the smells of so many weres are giving me a headache. I can't say I'm a fan of being pressed into a crowd like this. And I don't know where the action is going to take place, but there's a very good chance I won't be able to see it unless they decide to do it standing atop the bar.

In an attempt to calm myself, I pull my hair into a braid and wrap that into a bun, securing it with a pen from my purse. I turn my wool cap inside out, hoping to dry the inside before I have to put it back on and go out into the freezing Alaskan weather. I feel a bit less strained for a minute, then someone I don't know backs into me and tramples my foot; and just like that I'm back on edge again.

A millisecond before I make a break for the door, a whistle prompts an eery silence. Then a voice says, "We're moving outside, people. Meet in the lot across Pine Street."

It's a relief for me to be hustled and bumped to the exit, but I hear several people complaining. I'll admit that had I known I'd be standing outdoors, I would have worn an extra layer or two of clothing, not to mention taken the time to dry my hair a little better, but I'd rather be cold than continue locked in a press of bodies. I yank my cap on inside out and wiggle my hands back into my mittens.

We all cross the road to an unused lot full of snow, making me glad I threw on my boots rather than something less hardy, and Lyly drags me through the crowd until we're on the innermost layer of the circle that forms around some old woman I don't know and the Pack leader, Winston Denali. Lyly holds her clipboard up in a mittened hand and calls for Mr. Denali's attention. "I have a petition-"

"Yes," he cuts her off, the clipped word going well with his sophisticated-older-guy looks. "I'm aware of it. You'll have a chance to speak in just a minute."

Of course he's aware of it. Warren would have told him already, although I'm not sure what Warren's opinion on the matter is. I mean, I'm sure he wants Troy as far away from Michaela as possible, but at the same time, wolves seldom argue with their mates, especially when the couple is newly established. He and Michaela stand across the circle from us, whispering to one another. I can't tell a thing from the shaggy-haired, blond wolf's expression, but his mate seems unusually calm. Almost serene. Simone would want to claw her eyes out. Despite her shoulder-length brown hair looking like a rat's nest and her pale skin glowing red with cold, Warren regards her with a look of absolute worship. She's not conventionally pretty, but I have to admit that there's something about her people just respond to.

As the wind whips through the field, I reach a hand to my hat. There's a crisp layer where the water has turned to ice.

The crowd falls silent and parts in an almost mystic way, and Troy walks through the gap, flanked by two wolves who, I think, work as bar bouncers. If they don't, they certainly could. Troy isn't a small person, but they dwarf him. If being pinned between a pair of hulking beasts makes Troy at all nervous, however, he doesn't show it. His calm stops just shy of cockiness.

The wolves haven't bothered to restrain Troy, but I can't tell if that's because it wouldn't matter, or because Mr. Denali wanted to make a point about not considering Troy a threat. Wolves can be much more devious than people give them credit for.

"Troy Millerton," booms one of the escorts.

The crowd closes behind Troy, and he glances around. His demeanor shakes a little, but he keeps ahold of himself. Knowing he can fly out of here any time he wants to change into a bird must be comforting. If I were in his place, I'd be just about terrified. In fact, I can taste the fear at the back of my throat just thinking about it.

"How do you plead?" Mr. Denali asks.

Troy startles a little. "Um... you haven't told me what I'm charged with."

Warren steps from his place at his girlfriend's side. "He admits to wrongdoing, but begs leniency by virtue of cultural ignorance."

"Like hell, I do."

The guys glare at each other, and I swear I see Mr. Denali's mouth twitch like he's holding back a smile.

Warren closes his eyes for a second before asking, "So you don't admit you turned two human girls into all-weres like yourself, or you don't want leniency?"

Inching closer, Michaela whispers, "Don't be an idiot, Troy. He's trying to help you." She's new enough that she keeps forgetting the people around her all have better hearing than regular humans.

"I turned them," Troy mutters. "And I recognize that I shouldn't have done it without permission. I'm sorry."

He looks up at Michaela as he says the last, seemingly sincere.

"Very well," says Mr. Denali. "Guilt has been established. I'll hear arguments for punishment now."

"Death!" someone yells. The crowd shifts to let a short, stumpy woman through. "Lance did the same thing and died for it. So should this boy."

Mr. Denali nods as though that was reasonable and a large portion of the crowd cheers, a few growling in anticipation.

"However," Warren says quickly, "Lance was raised here and knew the rules. Troy's parents are not weres, and he had no community to teach him. By sending him to North Pole, we can see that he is educated-"

"We can do that here!" Lyly bursts out. She stomps forward, petition in hand. "We have a school, and it's full of people who are willing to welcome Troy into our community. Surely that's better for his rehabilitation than being sent to live with a bunch of criminals."

Warren watches Lyly as he takes a deep breath. "The residents of the North Pole Center aren't criminals. It isn't a jail. It's a rehabilitation center, specifically designed to educate those who need it."

It occurs to me that he's being a little more articulate than usual. Not that he's usually stupid or anything. Just that he usually sounds like a normal person, and he doesn't now. Was this whole thing rehearsed, or is he just channeling the spirit of a lawyer?

"And what's a school if not a place designed to educate?" Lyly counters. "Or should anyone new to the were-community be sent to North Pole rather than allowed at North Sky?"

Everyone watching turns their attention to Michaela for a second. She squares her jaw and ignores us, continuing to keep her eyes on Warren.

"And have you asked the school their opinion?" Mr. Denali interrupts. "Are they willing to house someone who would change people against their will?"

Lyly smiles. "It's not like he can turn any of us. And, yes, I asked the school and have a petition here."

One of the bouncers takes the clipboard and gives it to Mr. Denali, who frowns as he reads it. "This isn't the entire student body."

"No," Lyly admits. "We didn't have time for that."

Michaela takes a step forward. "You will note my name is there, sir. As the one who he turned, I think it is safe for him to stay here. I've forgiven him and don't think he needs more punishment. He's already been in exile in the wilderness for weeks."

A slow smile spreads across Troy's face, and I can't help but assume he's reading a bit too much into what she's saying.

The woman who spoke first lets out a wail of frustration. "Why are we listening to these children? They're not even Pack!"

In a flash, Warren's expression goes from composed to viscous. "Michaela is Pack as long as I'm Pack."

Mr. Denali holds a hand up toward his son. "That aside, this is more than a Pack matter, Helen. This affects all of us. That's why the Den is here, and why the other groups would have sent agents had there been time."

The old woman next to Mr. Denali nods. "Rather than take offense at the notion that my opinion means nothing because I'm a fox, I'd like to move along. I believe there are three options before us. Execution, imprisonment, and... school."

An idea suddenly hits me and I find myself stepping forward. My fingers tingle with nervousness as attention shifts to me and I start to wish I had a blanket to hide under. "What about his family?" I make myself say, forcing myself past the urge to vomit. "They're going to be looking for him, and eventually that will them lead here. What will we tell them if he's dead?"

There's a grumble from the crowd, and Helen turns to me with a scowl. "We tell them we don't know what they're talking about. There's no proof he's been here."

"I won't."

Everyone stares at me. I'd be staring at me too if I could. As it is, I swallow my nervousness and take a breath to clarify. "If you kill him, I'll tell the humans. So you'll have to kill me, too."

"And who are you?" Helen asks.

But I don't have to answer her question because a chorus of people saying, "Me too!" crops up to drown out anything I'd say.

"Let me be very clear." Mr. Denali says slowly. His eyes reflect the dying sunlight to look like they're on fire. "I don't respond to blackmail."

"However," says the matronly vixen at his side, "we do take public opinion into account. And I agree with them, Winston. The boy doesn't need to die."

Mr. Denali nods sharply. "Very well. Then we're down to two options. Unless someone wants to try to manipulate that."

Shivers race across every inch of my skin as Mr. Denali's eyes narrow on me. And the shivers don't let up just because he looks away again a moment later.

Lyly points at her petition. "That's not all I have, sir."

"Oh?" Mr. Denali's lips press together as he looks to Lyly, who pulls a letter from her pocket and hands it to him. He unfolds it, and his breath whistles in as he reads. "It's an official invitation for enrollment from Principal Atherton."

The wolves shift uncomfortably at the name. Our principal used to be Pack, but was exiled by the leader before Mr. Denali for something or another. I never figured out what because they don't talk about it. Whatever it was, it was apparently bad enough for excommunication but not bad enough for him not to be trusted with the education of my generation.

The elder fox puts her hand on Mr. Denali's arm. "It's not like we can force the boy to stay at the camp anyway."

"Our children are at that school!" someone objects from the rear.

"So are my grandchildren," says the fox, her voice calm and her gaze steely. "But I don't believe this boy is a threat to them. He hurt two people under very specific circumstances, and I don't believe they shall repeat here."

"No," says Troy, very quickly. "Never again. I swear."

Mr. Denali nods. "Very well. We'll have a sorcerer in to bind you to that promise, but then we shall enroll you at North Sky."

A sorcerer? I hold back an exclamation. Sorcerers are expensive and of questionable use. A strong enough will can override anything a sorcerer tries to inflict on you, but I can hardly argue against it, can I? Not when that could put the execution option back on the table.

I stuff my hands deep into the pockets of my parka and hope I didn't royally screw up.

Chapter Three

Sunday creeps like a lethargic snail. Like many a morning, I wake too early and can't get back to sleep. So I sit in my room watching black-and-white movies until lunch, which I skip to check in with Nurse Sakura.

I find the coyote curled up on her waiting-area sofa watching anime. She pauses the show as I walk in and gives me a smile. "Hey, Rina. What's up?"

Looking around the room, it would seem like despite being solidly in cold and flu season, nothing is up. "I just thought I'd check and see if you needed help today."

She laughs and repositions herself to take up less of the couch. "Not exactly. But if you're up for Miso Maho Doki Doki, I'll turn the subtitles on for you."

Coyotes are, obviously, from the Americas, but Nurse Sakura is half-Japanese and spent a lot of summers there with her grandparents. She was in college in Arizona when she was turned into a were by what she describes as "an overly-enthusiastic girlfriend."

I've never heard of Miso Maho Doki Doki, but I sit down anyway. "What's it about?"

"It's a shojo yaoi. These guys on the screen right now are culinary students, but in a world where food and magic are the same thing."

"And they're in love with each other?" I ask, taking a stab at the yaoi part of the description.

"Not these two. The one on the left is straight. Maybe. There's another guy he might be into, but he hasn't realized it yet."

I nod. That kind of thing can take a while to figure out.

Nurse Sakura brings up the subtitles and we settle into a few episodes before Aniu Nannuraluk comes in complaining of an upset stomach. The polar bear is unusually pale and holds her arms around her ample midsection. I spring up and grab one of the plastic emesis basins on the shelf by the window, because I'd rather be safe than sorry.

Aniu takes the kidney-shaped pan with a weak smile. And immediately requires it...

This means that when my older cousin pings me via text and tells me I absolutely have to try the new game she's playing, I'm quick to go. I don't mind being around sick people, but Nurse Sakura has everything under control. Online computer games aren't really my thing, but they are Evgeniya's, and I've been wanting to spend more time with her lately. Thus, I log onto the website she sends me even though the name Chibifae makes me nervous. I mean, role playing as fae just doesn't seem like the best idea in the world; what if it offends an actual faerie?

"Calm down," Evgeniya types in Russian when I express the concern. "There are faeries on here. They think it's hilarious."

I'm not sure if I should believe her or not, but I start making myself a character nevertheless. I pick something that looks like an anthropomorphic cat, make her fur pink, and dress her in archer's garb.

The next time I look at the clock, prompted by Evgeniya announcing she's going to bed, it's nearly three and time for my hengedo martial arts group to meet. As I get ready, I relish in not having to argue with Simone about going. Then I feel guilty, because I really do miss her. Overall.

I slide into the room and go on instinct to my usual corner, but find it occupied. Seth stands in it, looking a little lost as the people around us do warm-up stretches. Unlike the rest of us, he's dressed in loose-fitting clothes that look comfortable and allow a lot of movement, but give opponents too much to grab. If he stays with this, he'll want to get some of the tight gear most people wear for hengedo.

"Hey," he says, his eyes on Penny Appleton as she leaps into the air for a high spin kick. It's not a move we're allowed to use during combat in our discipline, but the frizzy-haired wolf has a tendency to show off for new people. Especially when the new people are cute guys. Of course, I would never call Seth cute, both because Simone would kick my ass and because it's a serious understatement. "Um... Mr. Billings said to wait here. Or is he sensei?"

The very thought makes me laugh. Hengedo is a hybrid system developed by werefoxes. Perhaps because it was invented by such small creatures, the teacher is considered only to have solely situational authority over students rather than the broader views of many other martial arts. "Actually, we usually call him Billy."

Seth's eyes narrow for a second before widening on Penny's next move, a backflip that would be more at home at gymnastics practice. If we had a cheerleading squad here, the petite black girl would be the one the others threw up for aerial contortions. "Am I expected to do that?"

It's tempting to tell him that he most certainly is, but I take pity. "No. In fact, if you do it in a bout, you'll be disqualified."

He looks relieved, but I'd bet he could do if if he tried, judging by some of the things I've seen him pull off on skis in the terrain park.

Billy comes in before we can talk about anything else, and walks up to us.

"Seth," he says with nod. "Rina, I want you to take him under your wing today." I swallow nervously, but return the nod. "What's first?" the were-tiger prompts me.

"Falling!"

The answer earns me a wide smile. As the deep lines on his face attest, Billy is quick to smile. He's got an approachable grandfatherly thing going for him that translates to all us hengedo students adoring him. "Get to it. We'll be starting soon."

He leaves us and I turn to Seth. "How much do you know?"

"Um..." He puffs his cheeks and blows out a breath. "Don't brace. Keep your chin tucked. And, um..."

"Those are the main things. Along with staying loose in general. But I'll demonstrate." I wave Penny over. "Do me a favor and give me a toss?"

"My pleasure, M'Lady," she says with a grin, before lashing out lightning fast to flip me to the ground.

I land properly, then spring up. "That's it! You wanna see it again or are you ready to try?"

His eyes are nervous, but he tells me, "Go for it."

I shove him backwards. He lands almost-perfectly, but stays down for a bit, as though I've stunned him.

"You okay?" I ask, holding my hand out to help him up. He takes it and climbs back to his feet with a shaky smile.

"Seeing you in a different light is all." He grins. "Alright. Again?"

"Sure." I sweep my leg out, flooring him again.

He laughs from the mat, but before I can ask him what he's laughing about, Billy whistles for our attention. Obediently, everyone hops into two lines, facing each other. I make sure to place Seth beside me rather than in front of me. This way he'll be paired with Jonathan instead of me. Jonathan has only been coming to these things since fall, and he's a tiny little freshman, so Seth might stand a chance against him.

Usually, no one really wants to face me, but today Penny leaps into the position. She holds a hand up to cover the left side of her mouth, the side that Seth is on, before mouthing, "What's he doing here?"

Us cats are the ones who are supposed to be curious, but Penny has never let being a wolf stop her from nosing into things that are none of her business. I give her a shrug that I know won't satisfy her and drop into the ready position that precedes the kata, or sequence of poses we use to warm up. Sure enough, her dark brown eyes narrow on me as though my response was completely unsatisfactory.

In my peripheral vision, I see Seth struggling to keep up with the rest of us. Maybe giving him an inexperienced mirror was a bad call. Still, I think he'll thank me when he realizes he's going to have to spar with the guy across from him.

As per our usual pattern, we slide from our poses into waiting, and from there we begin a series of quick combat drills. Most of the pairings end with Billy calling halt, but there's always at least one that concludes with someone on the ground. I'm expecting that one to be Seth's until he and Jonathan start.

It's clear from the beginning that Jonathan knows more about the techniques we use, while Seth is struggling to translate the earlier poses into useful moves. Despite that, Seth's quickness and agility keep him from being dominated. I'm particularly impressed with the aikido roll he pulls off, seemingly from instinct as I didn't teach it to him.

The spar between Penny and me should be close to even, except she keeps looking over at Seth, which allows me to flip her onto her back in just under a minute.

"Alright," Billy snaps. "Circle up!"

Obediently, we form a circle around him and all drop into a sitting position facing the walls for our five minutes of meditation. Five minutes isn't really long enough, but those of us who benefit from it tend to meditate on our own. I would have earlier if I hadn't gotten so caught up in the new game.

I settle into my mind, quickly reaching a state of tranquil acceptance. Beside me, I hear rustling from Seth's direction. Even five minutes is a long time to sit perfectly still if you're not used to it.

The rest of class passes normally until our second round of sparring, when Billy decides to pair me against Seth even though I'd gone out of my way to avoid it earlier. At least this time, we don't go pair-by-pair, but all at once, so no one else has to see me tossing him around when it's time for that.

As in aikido and judo, much of the emphasis in hengedo is on getting the opponent on the ground. There's also a lot of jiu jitsu in hengedo, which means much using your opponent's momentum against them. So when Seth lashes out with a karate-style punch, I step into it with a slight turn. Then I simply grab his wrist and use it as a fulcrum to flip him down over my shoulder.

"What was that?" he asks, confused, as he climbs to his feet.

I flick my ponytail back out of my way. "Shoulder throw."

"And how did it happen?"

Laughing, I repeat the motions against an imaginary opponent. Seth tries to copy me, but doesn't come close until I've thrown him three more times. Maybe I'm starting too hard....

Backtracking, I teach him a couple of simple blocks and cuts, followed by a few very basic kicks. He holds back a little, but I'm hoping that's just from being new. A lot of newbies make the mistake of not using enough power, because they're scared of hurting themselves or others.

"I knew you'd take to this teaching thing," Billy says with a smile before making some minor adjustments to Seth's stance and moving on.

"You're good," I say as I block a punch. "But are you sure this is going to translate to cat-form?"

"Not really." He blocks my counter, which I deliberately slowed down to let him do. "But it's going to have to. There's only one moon between now and the Challenge."

Which means that he only has three days he can assume cat-form to practice in that skin.

"Are you sure you're ready? I mean, can't this wait?"

He shakes his head and makes another jab at me. "Not if I'm going to respect myself."

All I can think to do is sigh. I'm never going to understand males. As far as I'm concerned, he could let Simone know but not officially challenge her father until an actual date is set for the wedding. I mean, Simone's dad is still really strong, but he's only getting older. Surely he'll be easier to beat in five years than today.

Seth catches the sigh, as evidenced by a tightening in his jaw. "Remember what Polonius said."

"Yeah, yeah." I can take a guess at which quote he means. "Above all, to thine own self be true." I deliver a swift kick that sends him sprawling backwards. "But remember what happened to Polonius."

He smiles up at me from the mat. "He only died because he thought hiding behind curtains to eavesdrop was a good idea. I plan on avoiding curtains."

I can't tell if he's being cocky and overly optimistic, or just confident. I want to believe in him, but I'm not sure if I can let myself do it. Not when I know how upset it's going to make Simone.

I go from practice to running to showering, so by the time I'm ready for dinner, most people have eaten already. I take the cooked entree of the evening, a shepherd's pie, and go to my usual table even though there's nobody at it.

After a few minutes, I hear someone walking behind me, and look back to see Troy approaching.

"Can I sit here?" he asks, jerking his head toward the seat across from me, the seat Simone usually sits in. "You're the only person I know who's here right now."

"Sure." I watch him as he sits, taking in the changes since the last time I saw him. He's cleaned up considerably and smells a lot better. The scraggly hair on his face has been removed and his jeans and North Sky hoodie are both spotless. His scent is strong, but much more pleasant than it was yesterday. It makes me ever so slightly dizzy, in a good way that I try to ignore. It's strange; I usually don't react this strongly to boys, just girls.

He's also taken the cooked meal. Most people do.

"So, are you bound yet?" I ask.

"Yeah." He shudders. "That was the most freakish thing that's ever happened to me."

"Really?" I feel my eyebrows go up. "Weirder than turning into an all-were?"

"Well, yeah." His eyes are on his plate as he speaks. "I wasn't attacked. Not that I remember, anyway."

"Still. Your family isn't were, right?"

"Not as far as I know." He mixes his food up some. "They don't smell like they are. But I didn't really understand that until I came here, because I never met other weres."

"You never tried to talk to them about it?"

He snorts. "No. Assuming they believed me, they'd sell me to the highest bidder."

"But they're your parents!"

"Yeah." His features are remarkably calm as he looks up at me. "Which means I know them."

My parents may have shipped me off to be fostered by strangers, but they certainly didn't do it for money. They did it as part of a peace treaty. By banishing me from home, they stopped a war. Nothing less important than that would have made them let me go. I can't imagine what it must be like to live with people who you're certain would sell you for cash.

"So where do they think you are now?" I ask.

He shrugs. "No idea. Despite what you said at the trial, I can't imagine they're wasting much energy looking for me."

"And the FBI?"

That strikes him as hilarious. "They're not going to tell the FBI. It would make them look bad. They're probably telling people I've been sent to boarding school."

"And I guess you have."

His smile doesn't have much humor in it. "Guess so."

We eat in silence until there's nothing left on our plates, at which point he asks me, "So, what happens around here on a Sunday night?"

"The skating rink is open, and the library and workout room always are."

He looks less than enthused with these options.

"There's probably a movie or some X Games coverage on in the common room. Maybe hockey."

His breath hisses in. "I'm not sure I'd really be welcome in the common room. People are giving me a pretty wide berth."

"Really? Usually people are all excited to see new students."

"Well..." He leans back in his chair, taking it onto its rear legs. "I'm going to go out on a limb and say most new students aren't considered criminals. They may have signed that little petition that girl had-"

"Lyly."

"Lyly. Okay, they may have signed Lyly's petition, but that doesn't mean they like me."

And I suppose it doesn't. "It's okay. I'm not terribly popular right now either."

"Why? What did you do?"

"Let my best friend be totally horrid to Michaela. She got suspended. I just got ostracized." Although, even as I say it, I wonder how true the statement is. It's not like I had a great many friends in the first place. People seem to like me well enough, but the only people I've really connected with here have been the other snow leopards.

"I can't imagine you being nasty to anyone."

I shrug. "It was more me going along with Simone being nasty, but I can't blame people for being upset with me."

His chair's front legs lower to the ground as he leans forward. "Have you talked to Mike about it?"

My eyes widen. It's not that the idea of apologizing hasn't occurred to me; it's more that I'm terrified of trying.

"She forgave me," Troy says. "Seems to me my crime was worse. You should talk to her."

"Maybe," I say. I'm pretty sure he's right, but it's going to take a while for me to work up the courage.

I sleep on the idea of talking to Michaela, but when I see her at breakfast I walk to sit by Amber and her new girlfriend.

"Good morning." Amber smiles at me as I sit down across from her and Raja. "Pray tell, is it true that my misguided fool of a sibling has been soundly beaten in combat?"

I laugh at the words, even though Amber's always been peculiar with phrasing. It's one of many ways she differs from her twin brother. She and Seth have the same facial structure, and if her hair was left natural rather than dyed black, they'd have the same hair, but both their eyes and the personalities behind them are completely different. "Not too soundly. He's got great instincts."

"Instinct shall not be sufficient against Rutherford."

No, it won't be. I look across the room to where Seth sits with his new friends. He's at the same table as Michaela, and might back me up if I went over there and things turned nasty. Or maybe he'd just get mad at me, too.

Raja reaches over to pat Amber's hand, her chestnut skin dark against the pale of her girlfriend's. "But it's not like Rutherford will kill him, right? Because that would destroy the alliance past the point where it could be renegotiated."

Even though Raja is a lioness, she has a decent handle on snow leopard politics and recognizes exactly how important the Seth-Simone match is to our peace. We're a bunch of small Clowders that have come together to form a modest-sized community, but without our alliances, we'd destroy each other. We came really close to it little more than a decade and a half ago.

"No," Amber agrees, nibbling on the side of a nail coated in shiny black polish. "But if he is defeated often enough, it will break his spirit."

I look back to him. He's laughing, apparently at something Samantha Fox said. "Well, then," I say, "we'll have to make sure he doesn't lose."

And now I guess I'm committed to helping him. My tea cup shakes as I bring it to my mouth. I feel like something really significant just happened to my life, and it makes me long to run away, even though Amber's relieved smile makes me want to stay. Amber is... special. And something in her orangey brown eyes always makes me feel like I am, too.

Seth really should have sent Amber to ask me to help him in the first place. I've never been able to tell her no about anything, even more so than Simone. You see, while Simone is like a sister to me, Amber is the first person I ever kissed, and sometimes I wonder if I ever got over her or if she just got over me. Not that Seth knows about the brief romantic relationship I had with his sister; as far as I know, no one ever found out. Raja may well know, but hopefully it doesn't bother her that we're still friends. Not that it should bother her. Nothing romantic has happened between me and Amber since I started high school two years ago. Besides, surely Raja is too gorgeous to have insecurities about things like that.

As I sip my tea, a text comes in asking me to check in with my counselor. So once I finish my cereal, I bid the happy couple goodbye and make my way through the building. On the way, I pass a few people. None of them make eye contact with me.

Chapter Four

The familiar scent of incense and candles meets me in the hallway. The door is closed tight, though, so I knock on it rather than walking in like usual. It opens quickly to reveal the smiling features of the woman responsible for my sanity. Young enough to pass as a senior, she's as much a big sister to me as a therapist, but both roles are important. When she smiles at me, there is a light of genuine affection in her eyes, hiding behind cat-eye glasses.

Against expectation, Becky isn't alone. Inside her cozy, lavender-infused room, Troy sits on the couch, looking surprisingly uncomfortable for someone surrounded by a mass of pillows. His lips move into a kind of weak smile, but his gaze hovers on the floor.

"Come in," Becky says with a wave toward the same couch that Troy is on. She's wearing one of her more hippie outfits today, a long skirt and flowing shirt done in earth tones that set off her dark skin beautifully. Meanwhile, I'm in my usual soft greys with my skin looking like mozzarella. As I settle hesitantly across the couch from Troy, I wonder why I didn't take the time to put on a little bit of makeup. Simone never lets me skip that part of morning preparations.

Troy's hair is damp, which tells me he showered this morning, yet his scent crests over the cornucopia of smells that live in Becky's office. It's a miracle his scent didn't lead every female in Alaska to him back when he was hiding out in the woods. It would be so easy to lose myself in it... too, too easy.

Becky clears her throat, raising her eyebrows at me as I slowly realize she's asked me a question. Expectation is obvious in her eyes, and I gamble it's expectation of an affirmative, so I nod. It seems to be the right response as her face brightens with a smile. "Good. I'm sure you'll be an excellent tour guide."

Her gaze lingers on mine, her eyes widening slightly. I interpret that to mean she knows I didn't hear the question but hopes I've caught on, so I nod a second time.

"Here's his schedule." She hands me a sheet of paper with a list on it. We actually have three classes together, which is a lot since I'm in the year under his.

She dismisses us without much ado beyond making sure Troy knows he can come back any time he needs to talk, and we head into the hallway. "Have you eaten?"

He grunts in a manner that's probably affirmative, but I go into the student kitchen anyway and turn on the hot water kettle to make myself another cup of tea. Troy takes some coffee and we set off through the building.

The first time I was here, North Sky seemed big and imposing to me. The only way that was possible, though, was because I'd been tutored by the adult members of my Clowders rather than sent to schools up through eighth grade. Now that I'm used to the place, I realize it's actually pretty tiny. No more than a dozen rooms inside and a few outbuildings make up the entirety of the chalet-style school, and since we stay indoors the tour is over before the end of first period.

Troy's lips turn up into a sort of sneer, crinkling his nose. "That's it? A hallway of classrooms, a library, and a gym?"

"And a music room!" I jab my finger toward the room in question. My school may be small, but it's not worth sneering at.

"A music room," he mutters, not sounding at all impressed despite it having a full-sized piano in it.

"There's more outside," I point out. "You're the one who asked not to see any of that. I bet your last school didn't have a skating rink."

He shuffles awkwardly. "I don't have a coat to go outside in."

"You don't...." The words make so little sense to someone living in Alaska that I have a hard time finishing the sentence. "How can you not have a coat?"

"Well, I did." With his back bent and his hands stuffed into the pocket of his hoodie, he looks unspeakably emo. "I threw it out. Freezing to death would be better than wearing that thing again."

"Oh." Right. He must have been wearing the same coat for weeks when he was doing the survival thing out in the woods. "There's a general store in town. Maybe we can get a ride there this afternoon."

"No money either." He shrugs like it's not a big deal. "I'll be alright."

Sure. Until one of his outdoor classes come along.

I make a mental note to go buy the guy a coat from the discount rack after school, but show him to our shared French class without telling him I'm doing it. Once upon a time, I would have asked Simone to ask Seth to take me, but not only is Simone gone, so is the car. It was never really Seth's, but the Clowder's. Theoretically, it could have gone to either me or Simone when he fell out of favor with her dad, but neither of us have driver's licenses yet. Of course, the license that Seth has says he can only carry family members. We always ignored that, so I'm not sure why it matters that we don't have a license at all. It's a challenge trying to guess which human rules my Elders expect me to obey and which ones they toss out.

Under the theory that I'll need Lyly to take me to the store later, I steer Troy to her table at lunch.

"Hey." She doesn't look at us as we sit down, being too busy staring across the room. I follow her gaze to a table where her ex-boyfriend, Tod, is sitting beside his current girlfriend, AKA Lyly's sister, Aliah. Does that suck, or what?

On the other side of the dining hall, Michaela appears with a tray of food and takes the seat on the other side of Tod. The move makes Lyly start to growl, but it's Troy who speaks. "So that's the fox guy, right?"

I nod and whisper back to him. "Their Den Father. And Lyly's ex."

The whispering doesn't do any good, of course, and Lyly hears me anyway. "My ex indeed. Because of that conniving cow and my brat of a sister."

"I'm lost," Troy admits. I should be so lucky.

"Look at them!" Lyly all but froths at the mouth.

I look, but they seem to just be talking, so I'm not sure what I'm supposed to be looking at. Warren shows up looking all ruggedly handsome and slides in beside Michaela, giving her a quick peck on the cheek. Hardly a scene to get upset about.

Except now Troy's making unhappy sounds too. "And that's the wolf."

"Warren," my mouth says before my brain realizes it would be better to keep quiet.

Lyly heaves a puff of air up to move the short fluff of hair that was encroaching on her eyes. "And Mike." She says the name with no small amount of hatred. "Perfect little Mike, who ruins everything she gets near. You'd better tell Seth to run."

Sure enough, Seth now sits at Michaela's table, right beside Tod's sister Samantha. They were next to each other at breakfast too. If I didn't know any better, I'd almost wonder if something was up between the two of them. As I watch Sam put her hand on Seth's shoulder, I start to wonder if I do know better.

I expect Troy to ask which one Seth is, but he doesn't. What he does is glare at Lyly. "If Mike Miasnikov did something to you, you did something to deserve it."

"Excuse me?" Lyly's attention snaps to our table, and her spine goes perfectly rigid. "You don't know me."

"And you obviously don't know Mike." He stands up, leaving his food on the table. "Thanks for everything, Rina. I'll see you around."

The sound Lyly makes as he departs defies description. It's somewhere between a snort and a hrumph. "What a loser. He's just as hung up on her as everyone else here. And to think I helped him stay here!"

I stuff a wad of lettuce into my mouth and wish I was the kind of person who knows what to say at times like this. I want to storm off with Troy, or maybe just go to another table, but it would take more guts than I have. Too bad the dining room isn't a martial arts studio; I always know what to do on the mats.

When I see Troy again, I walk timidly up to him, my eyes struggling to get off the ground but not doing a very good job of it. I mumble an apology, jumbling the words too much for him to possibly understand. I guess he understands the mood though because he gives me a little smile and a nod.

"No worries. Lyly's bitter about something. I get it. I just didn't want to listen to it, you know?"

"Yeah... She kinda thinks Michaela's the reason she's not with Tod anymore."

"Is she right?"

I shrug. "I don't know. It probably has more to do with the fact that she's broken up with him every month or two for years."

"This place is just a nest of drama, isn't it?"

Again, I shrug. "And your old school wasn't?"

I take my seat as class starts, and since he's assigned a chair across the room from me, that's all we can say until after class. By then, our minds have moved on to trigonometry and we talk about homework on the way to chemistry. There we're assigned as lab partners for the day. He's taking a sophomore class as a junior, but I soon realize it's not because he's an idiot.

Michaela's in chemistry too, backing up Troy's claim that it was a junior class at his last school. He spends a lot of time looking in her direction, but her attention never wanders from her own table. It makes me feel bad for the guy. I know what unrequited crushes are like, and can only imagine it's worse when you're talking about someone you used to date.

By the time the day is over, I'm feeling uncharacteristically tired, but I go to Becky's office to ask for a ride into town anyway. She gasps when I tell her why and promises to do it herself, so I take my run instead. Exercise and a shower later, I elect to make myself a sandwich in the student kitchen rather than deal with other people in the dining room.

The tactic works Monday evening, but when I try it again Tuesday morning, I'm foiled by Seth. He walks in, and I turn quickly to stare at the toaster. I will my bagel to jump out and let me escape lest he ask me why I let Lyly get away with bad-mouthing his friend. It's a paranoid thought, since he can't possibly know what we were talking about, but telling myself that doesn't make the fear go away.

"Morning!" He's too chipper for how early it is.

I mumble back an approximation of the same greeting, my eyes on the toaster, which still refuses to serve me my bagel.

"Not sleep well?" he asks.

I shrug. "Not a morning person."

"No, I guess you never have been." He pours himself a cup of coffee from the dispenser. "You doing alright this week?"

"Sure."

He laughs at me. "Yeah, that was reassuring. Want to try again?"

What does he expect me to tell him? That my best friend is suspended while my only other friend only has time for her girlfriend? That I have a choice between eating alone, being a third wheel, or putting up with Lyly's vitriol? "I'm fine, Seth."

The toaster makes a noise, teasing me although it's still not ready to give up my breakfast, and someone else walks into the room. Someone who smells like a fox.

"Morning!" says Sam. "You ready to ski? Tod says he'll take us early if you are."

"Sweet. Just grabbing a snack."

My head turns just far enough for me to see Seth, clad in his ski gear in preparation for the day, as he opens a granola bar and shoves about half of it into his mouth. I turn back quickly, before he can see I'm looking.

The pair leave with Seth tossing the quickest of goodbyes over his shoulder, and then the toaster finally gives me my bagel.

Chapter Five

The urge to go back to my room and watch movies all day is strong, but Becky got mad at me for doing that last week, so I get onto the bus that goes up to the ski slopes for the day with everyone else. I can't stand the thought of putting on my skis and going out alone on them, though, so instead, I go to rentals and borrow a snowboard and boots. Then I report to the snow sports school for a free lesson on how to use the silly thing.

Turns out the lesson was a really good idea. Despite how happy the instructor is to hear I'm a skier, I seem to have zero ability to snowboard. I keep trying to move my feet and end up with either my face or my butt in the snow. Then I spend a few minutes trying to get back up, all while wondering why boarders sit down as often as they do when it's this much of a pain to get up again.

Even though I'm abysmal at the bottom, the instructor takes me up the beginner lift anyway. It's a slope I can ski backwards without a second thought, but every time I start to move my body freaks out and does something to bring me down. It takes forever to get to the bottom, and by the time I do I'm too cold to even think about going up again.

I thank my instructor for the lesson and return my stuff, unsure if I wasted the day or not. I mean, at least now I know I don't like snowboarding.

On the walk across the base area to the coffee shop where everyone hangs out when they're done on the snow, a boarder slides over to me. The wind is blowing the wrong way for me to smell him, but when he pulls up his goggles, I recognize Troy. He's grinning for the first time since I've met him; it's a good look.

"Check it!" he says. "Atherton hooked me up with all this. Can you believe it?"

"Nice." I smile back, happy for him even though every new scholarship student gets the same deal.

He pops his foot from the binding and flips his board up into his hand, revealing a graphic of a fiery dragon. His eyes flicker to my feet, which are wearing my standard snowboots. "You done already? Didn't we just get here?"

I laugh at that. "It's lunch. And, yeah, I'm done for the day. Going to read at the cafe."

He shakes his head. "Silly little kitty. I'll eat with you, but then I'm hitting more slopes."

Technically, I didn't invite him to lunch, but I don't say anything to stop him trailing after me or taking his newly purchased meal to the same little table I sit at. The table is in the corner and the only sight directly visible from it is the bottom of the lift that serves the terrain park, yet people keep looking our way as we eat. Lovely.

From his seat, Troy has a better view of the terrain park than I do. "That albino chick's good," he says around a bite of roast beef sandwich.

I twist to make sure he's talking about Aliah, even though she's the only actual albino in the school. "Yeah. Who knew? She only started hitting the park like last week."

He snorts. "She's been there longer than that. And she's the boyfriend-stealer, huh?"

"According to Lyly." I look back to the remains of my food. There's still half a chicken salad sandwich left, but I don't think I'm going to be eating it. "I don't really know Aliah, or even Tod, really. I mean Lyly only really hangs with us when they're broken up. When they were together, they were pretty self-absorbed."

"So without him, she's exactly the same as she is with him?"

I chortle, though I feel bad for the reaction. "She's not that bad. She's just having a rough couple of moons."

"If you say so." He looks over to my uneaten sandwich, and I nudge it toward him. "Thanks. You're awesome."

I think this is the first time anyone has ever said that about me.

The words are still bouncing around my head several hours later, when I've made it back to school and am heading to the gym for my run.

The gym isn't empty. Rather, it is filled by the Dae twins.

"You're an idiot!" Amber yells at her brother, who stands there calmly taking her abuse. "You know what? Maybe you deserve to be killed fighting Rutherford!"

"No one's getting killed," Seth says. He reaches out to put his hands on his sister's shoulders, but she twists away from him.

"You could! You can't promise me you won't. People die in Challenges, Seth. They do!"

"Not for over a century. Dan Rutherford isn't insane. He knows killing me would start the war up again."

"And what if, in the heat of the moment, he forgets that?"

The twins stare at each other, and I start to creep backwards, hoping to get out before they notice me. But it's already too late. As I draw level with the door, Amber's eyes snap onto me. "You agree with me, do you not? Tell him he should wait."

"Um..." That doesn't seem articulate enough, but this is definitely one of those times when I could use a script. Last I heard, Amber was supporting her brother's choice. What happened to set her off today? "Well... I don't think Dan will kill him...."

"See!" Seth waves his hand as though I'd given him a bigger vote of confidence than I had.

"I just fail to see why it couldn't wait," Amber says. "For crying out loud, your eyes haven't even changed yet!"

Seth's jaw tightens at that. Snow Leopards are born with blue eyes which, over the course of childhood, slowly change to brown. Seth's are as blue as the day he was born, but drawing attention to that is... well, it's rather insulting.

I know I should keep out of it, but I find myself intervening further. "My grandfather's eyes never changed. He's ninety and had three kids."

Brown eyes narrow on me. "Bravo for him. Seth isn't ninety."

"No," Seth agrees. "If I were, I wouldn't have to fight because Simone wouldn't want to marry me."

"She might," I say, earning funny looks from both the twins. "I mean, once she gets an idea in her head, it's pretty hard to get rid of."

If it weren't for that, it seems like it would be an easy task to get her to back off Seth. Pretty as the blue eyes are, they are a defect. And his hair... I've always been oddly fond of it, but the way his fur's coloring pattern carries over to his black and white human hair is definitely not something most people would look for in a mate. And the good Lord knows she doesn't love him for his personality either, pleasant though that generally is. No, Simone wants Seth because she was told he belonged to her, and for no other reason. And I'm the worst friend in the world for acknowledging any of that, even just to myself.

I walk past the twins and climb onto my usual treadmill. "One thing's for sure though."

"Oh?" Amber plants her hand on her hip. "And, pray, what is that?"

"Exercise is good for people. Stop arguing and start running."

Amber rolls her eyes, turns on a heel, and leaves, but Seth gives me a smile as he gets on the machine next to mine. And I can't help but notice it's one of the smiles I rarely see, the one that's more real than what he offers Simone, and I find myself hoping I see it more in the future.

With a shake of my head, I start to run. Less thinking and more running is definitely in order.

The prescription works, and my head is feeling nice and clear when we switch from the treadmills to the exercise mats and start to spar.

After a few minutes, I allow Seth to throw me over his shoulder, but twist to hit the ground on my feet. "You're getting better at that," I tell him.

He shakes his head. "Not better enough."

"It's only been a week."

With my eyes on his face, I sweep my foot out to trip him, but he blocks me. He wouldn't have before today. "Good job."

His eyes crinkle in a smile, and suddenly I'm flying backward.

I laugh as I look up at the ceiling from my back. "Well done. You're a good student."

"Nah, I just have a brilliant teacher." He pulls me to my feet with a wink. "So, who taught you this stuff? Your cousin? Evgeniya, right?"

"Yeah, Evgeniya got me into it. Then Dan took over."

"Dan?" He goes completely still as he stares at me. "So I'm being trained by someone who was trained by the guy I'm fighting? Small world, huh?"

"Tell me something I don't know." I feint left, then move right and get a punch in. He continues to stand there silently until I feel sorry for hitting him and straighten into a non-fighting pose. "You need to stop?"

He blinks a couple of times and shakes his head. "No. Sorry. Just spaced out. I think I'd forgotten about your relationship to Dan Rutherford. Are you sure you're okay with this?"

It's a serious question, so I take a moment to reflect on it. Sure, Dan's my foster father, and sure I've spent more time in his house than in my parents', but... well, frankly, I think he's wrong trying to force his daughter on someone who doesn't want her. "If I had a problem with it, I wouldn't be doing it."

"You sure about that?"

Sure about that? "What do you mean?" I ask, a little taken aback. "Do I usually do whatever anyone asks me to do?"

He stares at the floor until I start to realize that the answer to that. Yes, I usually do what I'm asked to do, and it usually doesn't really matter who's doing the asking.

"I'm sorry," he says. "I shouldn't have said that. I just..."

"Just...?"

He locks his hands behind his neck, his eyes still on the ground. "Just, I don't want to take advantage of your good nature. That's all."

The wording doesn't quite sound like his. "Amber said something about you taking advantage of me?"

His responding wince tells me I guessed right.

"Well, you're not." I wish he'd look up from the floor, but he's more intent on it than ever. "If I just wanted to please people, I would have said no because that would have made more people happy. Especially Simone. Who, I remind you, is going to kill me if she finds out about this."

"Yeah, I know." He drags his eyes up to mine. They try to flicker away again almost immediately, but I somehow hold onto his gaze. "I guess I just can't think of any other reason for you to help me."

I let out a long breath. "Believe it or not, I actually agree with you ending the engagement. The marriage is politically a good idea and maybe it will even happen later, but it's not like you're going to fall for her just because your parents forced you to spend time together."

Continuing to look at him is too hard, so this time it's me who looks away. "She deserves to be loved, Seth. And if you can't do it, then she needs to be free to find someone who can."

The clock on the wall ticks off the seconds as we stand motionless on the mat. I start to count the clicks and make it to twenty before Seth speaks, his voice deep and slow. "You really do see the good in everyone, don't you? Even Simone."

My eyes snap to his face. "You mean, I see what I want to see?"

"No." He shakes his head. "You're not delusional. You know Simone isn't perfect. You know she's capable of doing awful things. But at the end of the day, you still think she deserves good things."

My arms fold tight against my rib cage. "Everyone does."

"Yeah." He nods. "That's what I mean. Most people don't think that way."

I shrug, not knowing what to say about that. Maybe they do and maybe they don't. So what?

"It's a good thing," Seth says. "You seeing good, I mean. Not everyone else... More people should be like you. It's just really hard for most of us."

"So, you hate Simone, but feel guilty about it?"

"I don't hate her." He rubs a hand against his chin. "I hate a lot of what she does. And I don't enjoy being around her. But I don't hate her."

"She'll be so happy to hear that," I say. Then I hold back an urge to slap myself over the sarcasm. "Sorry."

"No. She's your friend. I should respect that."

"She used to be your friend, too. Or did I imagine that?"

He lets out another sigh as his hand falls to his side. "No, you didn't imagine it. But that was a long time ago. We just grew up in different ways since then."

I would question what he means by that, but before I can, Penny and a pair of her wolf friends come in to lift weights. Seth and I look at each other for a few heartbeats, then slide wordlessly back into sparring.

Chapter Six

When I hear a knock on my door early Saturday morning, my first thought is that they've let Simone come back early. Then I realize she would have told me about that so I could make a big production of welcoming her, but all we've talked about the couple of times her parents have let her call me is how boring life in exile is. My second theory is that someone must have the wrong door. I answer anyway, peeking my head around the door to conceal still being in in my pajamas.

"Good morning, Rina!" Troy stands in the hallway, dressed for snowboarding and wearing a cheerful smile. "Get dressed. I got us a ride to the slopes."

It takes a minute for me to process the order with my groggy brain. "Ride?"

"Yep. One of the wolves. Madison? She'll take us, but she's leaving in twenty minutes, so hurry."

"Okay."

I close the door on him and start to get dressed. I'm halfway done before I realize I just mindlessly agreed to do something solely because someone told me to.

For a good minute, I stand still in the middle of my room and contemplate going back to tell Troy I'm not coming. But the problem with that is that I really don't have anything better to do with my day. I'm caught up on my homework, there are no sick people to take care of, and Evgeniya isn't going to be playing Chibifae because she's at some kind of theater retreat. Besides, I'd like to get some more practice snowboarding. It's embarrassing to be having troubles with the bunny slope, and once I got over being so cold last time, I realized I wanted to do better.

Firm in the belief that I'm doing it because I want to, not because I was told to, I finish throwing on my clothes and sunblock before going out to the hall to find Troy. He leans against the wall across from my door, his arms crossed casually and no sign of boredom on his face. If he had any doubt I was coming with him, he doesn't show it. That annoys me a little, though not enough to say anything about it.

We stop by the student kitchen just long rough for me to grab a granola bar and a jug of milk, then go wait by the door to the parking structure for Madison.

There's not much I know about Madison. I know what she looks like: tall, dusky skinned, wide hipped, and featuring hair that's a different color every few weeks. She's a senior, a wolf, and a painter. And I've said maybe five words to her the entire time I've been here. I'm pretty sure they were, "Hi. I like your work." Wait! No, I've also told her, "Sorry you're sick. Would you like some orange juice?" So there's that.

When Madison arrives, it's with Penny and two other wolves I don't know well. One is Penny's older brother, Thomas, and the other a senior named Marie. I think Marie and Thomas are dating, but I wouldn't bet money on the thought.

We pile into Madison's Forester, which technically doesn't sit this many people. I'm even less comfortable than last time I bummed a ride somewhere. What I wouldn't give to have the Clowder's car back.... things were so much better when it was just the four of us in the one car, even if the back seat, where I always sat, did have next to no leg room.

It's cold up on the mountain, colder than normal, but I go over to rentals and get a snowboard anyway.

"Why do you rent?" Troy asks when I come out of the rental shop.

"Because I don't know if I'm staying with this or not. I usually ski."

He nods. "I started out as a skier. Didn't take."

"Oh, it took for me." I look down at the board and its funny bindings. "I just wanted something different for a little while. That's all."

"Different?" Penny slides up on her half-fastened board. "Well, you've got a board and you're hanging with us commoners, so I'd say you've achieved that."

I squint at her, confused. "Commoners?"

"You know, non-leopards." She shrugs a little apologetically. "I've never actually seen you associate outside your little circle except for hengedo or when people are sick."

"So, you think I'm stuck up...?" I shouldn't let that get to me. Simone certainly wouldn't. Yet, the tears teasing my eyes aren't just from the chilled wind.

"I didn't say that." She looks to Troy for backup. "I didn't say that."

"Not exactly," he agrees.

Penny latches the chin strap on her shiny red helmet. "All I meant was that you usually talk to the same three people. I didn't mean anything beyond that. I've always figured you're just shy."

It makes me feel a little better, but brings a new warmth to my face. She did say "commoners" though... That word must have meant something, even if she's playing it off now.

"Anyway..." she draws out. "If you want some help, I'll go up the beginner lift with you and see how you're doing."

Even though I'm still bothered by that word (Commoners... like I think I'm above people?), I smile and nod. "That would be great."

It takes me only twenty minutes to get down the slope this time, an improvement brought about largely by Penny helping me figure out how to get from sitting to standing in a reasonable amount of time. It's still ridiculous how freaked out I get whenever I start to pick up speed, but at least now I'm upright more often than I'm flat out on the snow.

"You just need practice," Penny says. "Do you want to do that on your own, or do you want me to ride back up with you?"

Her expression makes it obvious which option she wants me to pick, and I go ahead and choose it. If I'm going to continue to look stupid, it's best that no one who knows me sees anyway.

I don't look too stupid the next run though. I don't think. The only time I fall is when I reach the bottom and try to slow down, so that's certainly good. I'd definitely describe myself as improved.

About the time I'm starting to fear turning into an ice sculpture, Penny reappears and invites me to lunch. This time, I accept without even the slightest fear that I'm only doing it to make someone else happy. I may be saving my life by going to warm up just now.

When I take my gloves off in the cafe, my fingers start to ache with that tingly pain that comes from circulation picking back up after you've been cold. I've never liked the feeling, but its familiarity is oddly comforting.

We grab sandwiches and hot drinks at the counter, then join Troy and the others at a table near the fire. The seats by Troy are both taken, so I wind up next to Penny and her brother.

"Guess what?" Troy says as I sit down.

"What?"

"Maddie says vampires aren't real."

I shrug. "Probably because they're not."

"As far as you know," Troy counters. "As far as most people know, werewolves are made up, too. And witches, faeries, and the Loch Ness Monster."

Madison shakes her head. "Only two of those are a thing."

"Three," Penny corrects. "Faeries are real. My mom knows one."

"Yeah," her brother says. "But Mom also believes in astrology."

"The fae exist," I say softly. "In Russia, everyone knows this. They control much of the countryside."

"Whoa." Troy leans back as he looks at me. "You have an accent."

"Well, yeah... I did live in Russia until I was six."

"It just popped up." Penny looks at me strangely. "You usually don't have one."

I shrug. "It comes out when I talk about Russia. Or to someone Russian."

Troy grunts. "I didn't even know you were actually from Russia until just now. I thought you were American."

I don't know if that's a compliment or not. It could be, or he could be accusing me of being a fake. Not knowing what people mean when they say things is the number one reason I'd generally rather watch movies than be with people.

The conversation slides on as Troy asks about more and more crazy beasts of folklore and mythology. He's happy to hear dragons are real, but bummed that Bigfoot probably isn't. I tune out some as his list gets into the crazier areas of Grecian lore and notice an entire table looking my way.

Seth drops his gaze quickly, turns his head, and tries to pretend he wasn't looking over here. Beside him, Sam waves at me. What in the world? Curiosity nearly draws me across the room, but my natural hesitancy keeps me in my seat.

Troy notices my distraction and looks over his shoulder.

Now it's Michaela who tries to act like she wasn't looking. Her companion doesn't wave though. No, Warren just continues looking at us like... I don't really know like what. He doesn't look jealous, or moody, or even interested. But if he isn't interested, why look?

"I'm going back out," Troy announces. And he's gone before anyone responds.

Chapter Seven

Over the next week, when I'm not helping Nurse Sakura deal with a minor stomach virus that's going around, I spend more time with Penny and her friends, who go so far as to wave both me and Troy over to them at lunch by Wednesday. Madison, despite being the oldest, is the people-pleaser of the group, always trying to make the others happy. The juniors, Thomas and Marie, are indeed a couple, but are past the googly stage that Amber and Raja are still in. Which is good since the reason I'm not hanging out with Amber and Raja is that they hardly seem to notice outsiders.

With an intense sense of disloyalty, I realize Friday that I'm not as excited for Simone's return as I ought to be. Nevertheless, I make my way to the art room and spend two hours working on a sign that reads, "Welcome Back!" It's ornate, glittery, and largely purple, just as she'd want it to be, but I can't shake the worry that she'll be able to sense the lack of enthusiasm behind its creation.

The worry turns to fear when she arrives Sunday, and I have to force myself to go out to meet her after she texts me that she's pulling up to the school. I do force myself though, making myself put on shoes so that I can go out to meet her mom's SUV and everything.

Simone steps out of the passenger side with a scowl on her face that doesn't go away when I hug her hello.

"Where is everyone?" she whispers in my ear.

I'm debating on what to tell her, since saying I'm the only person in the whole school who really cares she's back seems cruel, when the door opens behind me.

"Si-si!" calls Lyly. The fox runs over to pull Simone away from me and into a new hug. "About time you came back. I've missed sane company."

Si-si? When did that happen?

They start toward the door as Simone's mom, Eileen, makes her way to the rear of the SUV to start removing the bags stowed there. She yanks the strap of one over her shoulder and moves another to the ground at her feet, where I pick it up.

Eileen smiles. "Thank you, sweetheart."

"No problem." I smile back, honestly happy to see my foster mother.

"Don't let her fool you," she says. "She really did miss you. And it means a lot to her that you're still there for her."

"Of course." The answer is more mumble than speech and brings a look of sympathy to Eileen's face.

"It means a lot to me, too."

"She's my friend," I say simply.

Eileen closes the hatchback, then puts her spare arm around my shoulders. "I know, honey. But I know it gets hard to remember that sometimes. I'm her mom, remember?"

Parental approval notwithstanding, I still feel bad for being as relieved as I am disappointed when Simone disappears into her room with Lyly and shuts the decorated door behind them. She didn't even seem to notice the poster.

I tell myself it's okay. I wanted to go to hengedo anyway, and now I'm free to. But both Penny and Seth look at me with concern when I get there.

"You alright?" Seth asks. I notice he's found some tighter clothes since last week, but try not to pay the fact too much attention.

I nod and try to smile. "Of course. Simone's back!"

"And you're here?" Penny asks. "Did you have a fight? I'd expect you to be catching up with her."

"No, she's just tired." I don't know why I'm lying, but don't have time to second guess it before Billy shows up and gets things started. Going through the normal routine settles my mind quite a bit and leaves me feeling almost like myself when it's over.

When I get back to my room, I find Simone sitting on my bed, her eyes narrowed at the door in disapproval. "Where were you?"

In theory, I could get upset that she doesn't know my schedule well enough to know where I was, but if I got upset about things like that, I'd be upset all the time.

"Hengedo." I walk inside and Simone makes a sniffing noise.

"You smell almost as bad as an all-were."

It's a good thing I've been long-conditioned not to take offense at little jabs like that. It's probably also a good thing that I don't consider female all-weres to stink. I mean, they smell unusual, sure, but it's not bad really, even if it's nowhere near as yummy as the scent of the males.

Simone flops back onto my bed like it's her own. "You're going to have to shower before dinner, or I'm not eating with you."

I bite back a comment about how I wasn't expecting her to notice my existence today anyway, and stick my tongue out instead. "I'm already on my way. See, I'm getting closer to the bathroom as we speak."

"Good girl." She pulls her phone from her pocket and starts to read something as I gather clean clothes.

The shower is fast, but thorough enough to remove the scents of the people I sparred with. It was lucky Simone couldn't pick Seth's out of the collage. I'm going to have to be careful not to run into Simone after one of my and Seth's one-on-one sessions. Assuming I can keep them up at all with her back.

All clean and dressed in the sweater Simone picked out for me last time we were in Anchorage, I exit the bathroom. Simone still lounges on my bed, but she's rolled onto her stomach and her socked feet kick back and forth as she types something on the phone. Her long blonde hair trails down her back, looking enough like mine that we could be sisters in truth, except hers is always tangle-free and mine is generally a mess. She smiles at me when I enter, finishes her typing, and flips over to sit up. "You're out! Good! I'm starving."

I'm not really hungry yet, but an early dinner is alright with me.

"Should I get Troy?" I ask. "Would you like to meet him?"

She stands slowly, her face stoney. "Why would I? I've heard all about him, and he's clearly a waste of time."

Oh. "He's not so bad."

"Whatever." She drapes her arm around my shoulders and steers me toward the door. "I haven't seen you in two weeks. You need to tell me everything I missed."

"Well..." She doesn't seem interested in Troy, and I can't tell her about training Seth. "I went snowboarding some."

"Snowboarding?" Her nose crinkles. "Why would you do that?"

I shrug. "I wanted to try something different."

"Uh-huh." She gives my shoulders a squeeze. "You mean you didn't want to ski without me."

"Maybe..."

Her head leans against mine for a second before she lets go of me to make it easier to go down the stairs. "It's alright, kitten. I'm back now and you don't have to be alone anymore."

Yet when we get to the dining room, we sit with Lyly and the two of them start talking to each other without letting me get a word in anywhere. If I vanished from the room completely, I'm not sure either would notice. I feel more alone than I have all fortnight.

Chapter Eight

Troy and I leave AP French together. I'd be impressed he's taking it as a junior if not for the obvious detail that I'm taking it as a sophomore. It's my fourth language, behind Russian, English, and Spanish. I don't remember learning Russian, but the others weren't hard for me. I guess I'm just lucky with languages. It certainly isn't a mark of intelligence, if my struggles in math reflect anything.

"So..." he says as he falls in beside me. "Do I get to meet this notorious friend of yours sometime?"

"You mean Simone?" I ask it as a stall. She really doesn't seem to want to meet him, but it would be rude to say so.

"Yeah. Unless you have other friends who got kicked out of school but are back now."

"No, just her..."

"And?" He bumps his shoulder against mine. "You're going to introduce us at lunch?"

"Why?"

"Why?" His eyebrows go up at the rather rude question I just blurted. "Because I can't date every girl in this school if I don't meet every girl in this school."

I roll my eyes. "Simone's pretty set on Seth."

"Yeah, but he's not set on her. I might be new here, but even I know that."

He grins at me as I try to figure out if he's really interested in Simone or not. As far as I know, he hasn't met her, and he's seemed pretty hung up on Michaela up until now, so I conclude he's joking in some weird guy way I don't get.

"Chill," he says. "I'm not going to steal your girlfriend."

My cheeks instantly flash heat, and I'm certain I turn beet red. "She's not my girlfriend. She's not gay."

His eyes slant to me. "She isn't? But only her?"

"If you really feel you should know," I confess, "I'm bi." Then I wonder what in the world made me say that. It's not something I've ever told anyone, although I assume Amber has it figured out.

He whistles. "That's good to know. Any other bi girls around here?"

His eyebrows wiggle in a playfully suggestive fashion that gets me to smack him. Why do guys all think bi girls are into threesomes? I may not have come out before, but that's exactly the response I was expecting.

"No, really, though." He pulls me to the side of the hall and gives me a serious look. "You're sure there's nothing between you and this Simone chick? Because I'm not sure I buy it."

"I'm sure." Nothing I can think of saying would make things better, so I stay quiet on the issue until I can slip into history with a quick goodbye.

As I take my usual seat between Simone and the window, I realize I'm still blushing.

"What's wrong with you?" Simone asks, voicing the question I was on the verge of asking myself. "You look sunburnt."

"I'm fine." I press my hands against my cheeks. Sure enough, they're giving off so much warmth they could be radiators. I try thinking about ice.

"Right." She looks toward the door. "Who were you talking to? Was it a guy?"

Still trying to force myself back to my normal color, I just shrug and continue to imagine rolling around in the snow. I can't believe I just came out as bisexual to someone I've known for a couple of weeks after keeping it secret from everyone else since I realized it back when puberty hit. It's almost like Troy used some kind of truth serum on me or something.

"Oh my God, that look!" Simone gasps. "It was a guy! And you have a crush on him! Who is it?"

She looks around the room. "No one followed you in, so he's not in our class... It's not Kevin, is it? Because you two would be totes cute together."

"What?" Kevin? I have a dim acquaintance with the only Kevin in the school, who is a senior I have nothing in common with except for studio art. "No. I was talking to Troy. But I don't have a crush on him!"

She snorts. "I should hope not. But you're keeping something from me. What is it?"

"I'm not," I insist. Which is technically true as it's not one something I'm keeping from her, but multiple somethings. "Honest."

Her expression is more than mildly dubious, but class starts before she can hound me for more lies. By the time class ends, talking about the Black Plague has successfully cleared my thoughts and appears to have made Simone forget what we were talking about. I thank God on both accounts as we head to the dining room.

We make it through the lunch line while it's still short and head for our usual table. I catch Madison watching me and give her a little wave which she, reluctantly it seems, returns. I hope she doesn't think I was just pretending to like her and the other wolves last week.

Simone preens herself as soon as she sits, making me realize Seth is in the room. He sits in his new usual spot by a vacant seat I know is reserved for Sam. "Why's he over there?"

"Um..." I shift awkwardly but can't avoid the question. "He's been sitting with them lately. And Amber's been with Raja..."

"Yeah, about that." She picks up her diet cola and pops it open. "Lyly told me about them going to the Valentine's Dance together, but how the heck did we not know she liked girls?"

"I don't know." Or I don't know how Simone never figured it out, at any rate; it always seemed pretty obvious to me, even before Amber kissed me. "But it's not like she ever crushed on guys or anything."

"So?" Simone waves her free hand through the air as the other one brings the can of cola toward her face. "Neither do you, really. But you're attracted to them. I mean, I've seen you watch them in gym class."

I shrug. She's got a point, I guess. My attraction to my own gender aside, I've never doubted that I was attracted to certain males. Yet I've never pursued one. Kissed at a party, yes, but that's been the extent of it.

Speaking of attractive males, I spy Troy walking toward us with a self-confident swagger and a tray full of food.

"What are you doing?" Simone demands as he lowers his tray to our table.

"Sitting down," he says. But he stays standing as he says it.

"No. You're not. Not here."

"Simone," I whisper. I want to protest louder, but I'm too busy being mortified. "You're being rude."

"I'm being rude?" She turns to me, her eyes wide. "He's the one trying to crash our table."

"Um..." My gaze flicks to Troy, who watches me in silence. "I may have invited him."

"Well, I'm uninviting him then." She looks back to him and makes a shooing motion with her hand. "This is an all-were free zone. Sorry."

Troy shrugs. "Whatever you say, lady."

I stare at his back as he takes his tray over to the wolves and sits in the place I was sitting last week. He doesn't so much as glance back at me.

"Honestly, Rina!" Simone shakes her head. "I leave for two short weeks and everyone goes crazy. You know better than to talk to him. He's the reason Kim's dead."

And here I was thinking Kim was dead because she went on a livestock killing spree and tried to frame someone else for it. I could have sworn her death was an execution ordered by the Unified Council, but apparently I'm crazy. I wish I was the kind of person who could say all that out loud. Then I could tell Simone outright that she's being a bitch. Maybe I could even storm across the room to sit with my new friends....

Lyly shows up and the conversation rushes away from me, which is probably a good thing. I stay quiet as the other two talk about how awful everyone else is. The fox really brings out the worst in Simone, but I've never found a way to get rid of her other than waiting for her to hook up with her boyfriend again. And since her boyfriend is currently staring lovingly at her sister, I don't think he's going to come to my rescue any time soon.

It's hard for me to eat, but I do it as I try not to listen to the conversation at my table.

I excuse myself early, telling the others that I have a few equations to finish before chemistry starts. I don't really, but I get my books and go into the classroom anyway. The teacher, a polar bear named Ms. Dobbinson, gives me a funny look as she reads a book at her desk, but she doesn't say anything as I take my seat and sit staring out the window.

A few moments later, Troy comes in and sits beside me. It's Simone's seat, but he's been there for the last week.

"Don't worry," he says. "I'll move before she gets here."

I shake my head. "I'm sorry, Troy. She's just really resistant to change, you know? She'll come around if you give her time."

"Yeah, but why would I do that?"

The bald question leaves me speechless.

Troy shakes his head and holds up a hand. "Look, you're a good person. And you've been as close to a friend as I've made here. But she's too much. I thought people were exaggerating about her, but no. They really weren't."

"It's defensive," I say quietly. "New things scare her, make her uncomfortable."

"But it's not just me, is it?" He puts an elbow on the lab table and leans over it. "Or are you going to tell me that those two weren't sitting there trash-talking everyone in the room while you were struggling to keep your food down?"

Why is he so perceptive? I wouldn't have suspected it from someone with his backstory.

"Look." He reaches out and takes my hand. "I just don't want to see you as a mindless lackey, alright? You're worth more than that."

Over at the door, a group comes in, and he quickly lets go of my hand, gives me a sad smile, and moves to the back of the room.

A lackey? I don't want to see me as a mindless lackey either. But it goes back to what Seth was saying the other day, doesn't it? When he said I do things because people ask me to. I do things because I'm expected to. And today I was expected to back Simone. Which I did, even if only by staying silent.

As I wait for Simone to come in, I rehearse things I could say to her to get her to come around about Troy. Is there a point though? Even if I got up the nerve to say something, Troy may not be willing to accept an apology from her. Apology? From Simone? Good grief, I must be losing my mind.

The idea of going mad is oddly appealing.

I startle as the chair beside me squeaks from Simone sitting down. She laughs as she plops her books on the table. "You were definitely thinking about a boy that time. Who?"

"No, I was thinking about you."

"Me?" She leans close, her eyes narrowed. "You were daydreaming about me?"

"No." I let out a breath as I lean back. "I was just wondering why you hate Troy so much. I mean, Kim liked him. Shouldn't you give him a chance out of loyalty to her?"

"He got her killed."

"Did he?"

We stare at each other while she thinks about it. "If he hadn't been so obsessed with Stinky Mike-y, Kim wouldn't have done what she did."

"Or maybe she would have hated Michaela anyway. I know she was our friend, but she wasn't stable. You have to admit that."

She shakes her head, refusing to admit anything.

"Okay," she says as the bell rings to tell us to take our seats. "I'll try to be nicer to him for your sake. Because I love you. But you are not allowed to be crushing on him. Got it?"

"Oh, I'm not!"

She nods, but not like she believes me.

Survival Skills is far and beyond my least favorite class, mostly because, like Hunting and Tracking, it takes place almost entirely outdoors. I may have been born in Russia and raised in Alaska, but standing around listening to lectures in subfreezing temperatures still isn't something I'd do without being forced into it. Soon, the weather will warm up, but then we'll be stomping around in mud and pollen, which isn't an improvement as far as I'm concerned.

To make matters worse, the instructor decided early on in the first semester that Simone and I were to be separated. I've been resenting that all year, but suddenly I don't mind so much; it gives me a chance to slide over to Penny, who stands near some other wolves in a cute yellow parka that really flatters her dark skin tone. "Hey. Is that new? I could never pull off yellow, but it looks great on you."

Her eyes flicker away like she's considering not acknowledging me, but then she looks at me and smiles. "Hey. Yeah. Found it on end-of-season sale. You doing alright?"

"Yeah."

Her eyebrows go up a little. "You sure? You looked like you wanted to cry at lunch."

I want to tell her she's being absurd, but I was on the verge of tears at lunch, wasn't I? That's why it was so hard to swallow my food.

She makes a hissing sound. "And now you're wanting to again."

With a conscious effort to dry my eyes, I shake my head. "No, I'm fine. It's the wind."

Mr. Briar calls for silence long enough to tell us that we're learning how to look for caves today before leading us in a long sludge through the snow toward the nearest cliff face. It would be a better class if he wasn't trying to teach us about places we've been going for years. The caves he's leading us to are used as a local make-out spot. I've never actually visited them, but everyone knows where they are.

I trudge along next to Penny, relieved when the rest of the class gains a little separation from us. "Can I ask you a weird question?"

Her breath puffs out in a white plume as she shrugs. "Shoot."

"Do you think I'm a lackey?"

She stops and stares at me until I stop and turn back to look at her. "Who called you that?"

"Doesn't matter." I fold my arms across my stomach and drop my eyes to that snow. "What matters is maybe I am."

"No, you're not." Penny starts walking again, grabbing my arm as she passes by to pull me into motion. "You just happen to be best friends with a very strong-willed woman."

"You say that like you admire her."

"You don't?" She squints at me. "You can say what you like about her attitude toward life, people, and the universe in general, but no one can claim the girl doesn't know her own mind. There's something admirable in that."

"Yeah. It's a trait I could use more of, that's for sure."

Penny links her elbow with mine and draws close. I can't help but notice the curve of her breast as she leans against me to whisper, "I don't think anyone would be too upset if you siphoned off just a smidgen of hers."

We laugh, but I fall silent when I catch Simone looking back over her shoulder at me. I would hate for her to think I was laughing at her.

I disentangle myself from Penny, trying to make the motion look natural. "So you don't think I'm a mindless follower?"

"You're definitely not mindless." She stuffs her hands into her pockets and curls in around herself as a new blast of wind slams into us. "In fact, you're probably one of the smartest people I know. You just need to speak up more. Don't let people disrespect your friends, any of them."

"I did stick up for Troy. Later, but I did."

"And you always stick up for Simone, so you're good."

I search her words for bitterness, but don't find any.

"She's going to try to be nicer to him," I say.

Penny chortles. "Hard to be less nice without getting suspended again."

"She's on probation. She'd be expelled."

"Well..." Penny gives me a lopsided smile. "For your sake, I hope she manages to be civil then."

"Thanks."

Ahead of us, there's an increasing rumble of discussion, and the path is blocked after a few more yards. Penny and I glance at each other, shrug, and huddle close to the group.

As the wind whips at us again, I realize why we're stopped.

"Do you smell that?" Simone asks loudly. "It's another one of them!"

Another all-were? Could it be? It certainly smells like one, but couldn't it be Michaela?

"It's probably Mike," someone says, echoing my thought.

"It isn't," Simone answers. She stalks over to me and pulls me through the group. "Smell. That's not her. It's someone else."

I obediently sniff, but don't pick up any more clues than I had before. "I don't know. I'm not really that familiar with her scent."

"But he is!" Simone hisses, jabbing a finger toward where Tod Fox, our teacher's assistant, stands with Mr. Briar. She has a point there; in addition to being Lyly's ex, Tod is one of Michaela's closest friends. Tod scowls in the direction the scent comes from like he's really annoyed to be smelling it, and there's no reason he should be annoyed to smell someone who he adopted into his Den.

Simone yanks on me again, dragging me to the side farthest from the teacher and his assistant. "What does that tell you about your new friend?"

New friend? Troy? "Nothing. It's a female."

She rolls her eyes like I'm an idiot. "And how did every other female all-were we know of get that way?"

He turned them. I catch on to her implication with a shudder. "But he can't be the only one in the world. Maybe this is the were who turned him."

"Really?" She tilts her head and gives me a pitying look. "You'll believe just about anything, won't you?"

I peer into the wind and wish I could see a clever comeback on it.

"No. But you will."

My breath catches at the unexpected defense. I hadn't even realized Penny followed us until she spoke.

Simone pulls herself tall. "Excuse me? Was someone talking to you, wolf-girl?"

"You're not exactly in private," Penny comes back. "And you could be right about the situation, but there are other possibilities. Including what Rina just said. You're prejudiced against Troy. You want to think the worst of him, just like you wanted to think the worst of Mike. But they're not bad people simply because you don't like them."

A whistle pierces the air, followed by Mr. Briar bellowing the word, "Quiet!"

He waits until everyone shuts up and looks at him before speaking. "We are going to go back to the school. Quietly. We are not going to gossip along the way. We are not going to panic the other students when we get back. In fact, we are going to be silent the entire walk back to the buildings and if anyone other than Mr. Atherton asks you what happened out here, you are to tell them to mind their own business. Do you understand?"

We all shuffle about and moan, but when he repeats the words, "Do you understand?" we chorus, "Yes, Sir!"

63

But as I catch Penny's eye, I know we're both lying. The first thing we're doing when we get back is warning Troy.

"Alright!" Mr. Briar booms. "We're going to file into the Annex. And you're going to stay there until Mr. Atherton says otherwise."

There's a groan at that. The Annex is by far the least modern of our buildings and is only warmed by a small gas heater that won't have been turned on yet. Still, it'll be easy enough for me or Penny to slip away as we get close to it.

We start back in dutiful silence, Penny and Simone glaring at each other from either side of me as we trail behind most of the class.

Halfway there, a pair of footsteps come up behind my little group, and Tod ushers us to the side of the path. I sink into the higher snow and hope whatever he wants to say is quick. I'm well aware that every second we spend getting back to Troy is a second he doesn't know to be preparing a defense.

"You shouldn't tell him," Tod says in hushed tones. "If he has nothing to do with this, then his best defense is being honestly surprised when he's questioned about it."

"Duh," says Simone, her arms folded and her attitude annoyed. "Any other obvious statements you want to make while you have us stuck in a snowbank?"

"Yes, actually." He mirrors her folded arms and stares at her for a moment. "Welcome back."

It's not what I was expecting him to say. I was expecting a threat about treating Michaela better. But it's all he gives us before turning and rushing up to the group ahead of us.

Penny and I look at each other.

"Oh, please." Simone takes a hunk of my sleeve in her hand and pulls me back to the path proper. I stumble in the snow, yanking my arm free as I reestablish my balance.

"He's right," Penny says as she follows us.

"Of course he is," Simone snaps. "And I told you to stay away from that all-were. When are you going to learn to listen to me?"

Penny makes a grumbly sound. "You're jumping to conclusions."

"I'm relying on instinct." Simone accelerates away from us. "My leopard says not to trust that guy, so I don't."

Part of me wants to stay with Penny and another part wants to speed up to catch Simone. Instead of doing either, I wind up walking between them on my own. It makes me wonder about Troy, about how lonely he must have been in his old life. Lonely enough to be desperate, to turn two girls against their will. Why not three? The only argument I can come up with in his defense is that my gut says he didn't turn this one.

As soon as we're released, I tell Simone I need to work out. Then I change and put in my time on the treadmill. Seth comes in after the first mile and hops onto the machine beside mine.

"You okay?" he asks as he starts the jog into his warm up cycle.

I grunt out a "Sure."

"You're not," he observes.

Rather than respond, I jam my finger against the "increase speed" button and run faster. Obviously, I'm not in the best of head spaces, but why would he think I wanted to talk about it?

He respects my plea for silence and increases his pace without further comment. It's not until I finish my run and step off the machine that he even looks at me again. "Feel better yet?"

I take a long swig of water. "I don't know."

"But you don't want to talk about it."

"Not particularly."

He comes to stand next to me and drops into a stretch. "Alright. Just sparring then?"

"Sparring is good."

Except I'm really not in a teaching mood, so sparring turns into me throwing Seth around until eventually my natural sympathy breaks through my angst. Maybe I need to find a second student to pit against him when I get into moods like this.

"Sorry," I say as I hold my hand out to help him to his feet for the dozenth or so time. "I'm just... I'm worried for Troy. And pissed that everyone assumes he's behind this new all-were. And scared that maybe he is, and I'm a complete fool for trusting him."

"I get it." He squares off, waiting for an attack from me even though I'm not in position for one. "The doubt that maybe you're the one who's wrong and everyone else is right. I live with that doubt."

Yeah, I guess he does.

"Let's talk about something happier." I drop into a waiting stance, then immediately toss an easy-to-block kick his way. "What's up with you and Sam Fox?"

He winces as he blocks me. "Not sure that's happier."

"Oh?" The answer is unexpected. "What's wrong?"

"Not so much wrong as not-right." He punches toward me, and I twist aside, letting his momentum carry him forward so I can trip him with my foot. He rolls as he hits the ground, bouncing back up without assistance. "But it's mutual, so..."

"Sometimes people are just meant to be friends."

"Exactly." He lunges quickly, and I let him flip me to the ground. But I latch onto his arm as I fall and pull him down with me, then flip him onto his back as I spring to my feet. He shakes his head as he looks up from the mat. "I need to stop being so aggressive, don't I ?"

I laugh. "In romance, or in sparring?"

"Either." He smiles ruefully as he gets up again. "Both?"

"If you want to stand up to Dan, you're going to need to be more defensive, and wait for a good opening. But be careful, because he's going to try to make you think there are openings that aren't there." I grin. "And I'm not the person to ask about the other thing. Try your sister."

He rolls his eyes. "The only times I've caught her without her other half lately, she's ended up yelling at me."

"She's worried, that's all."

"I know." He shakes his head. "I just wish she'd be a little more supportive."

I nod. "She is pulling for you. She's just not showing it well."

"Yeah." He looks at the clock on the wall. "It's time for dinner."

Glancing up proves him right. "I need to shower first. Or Simone's going to smell you."

He looks at me for a long moment. "You could let her. She doesn't own you."

"No, she doesn't." I pull the tie from my ponytail and give my hair a shake. "But I don't want to hurt her either."

"Fair enough." He picks his water bottle up from the corner. "Thanks for this. I appreciate it."

I'd say that it's nothing, but we'd both know I was lying. So I just tell him that he's welcome, grab my stuff, and run to my room while praying not to run into my best friend.

Freshly washed, I go straight to dinner despite my fear that Simone is going to take one look at me and know where I've been. When I get there, it turns out my worry was for nothing, because Simone isn't in the dining hall. Troy is though, sitting alone at the side of the room.

I get my serving of chicken pot pie and take it to Troy's table, where he sits with downcast eyes. The tray hits the table, and his head snaps up. A slow smile spreads as I sit down.

"How you doing?" I ask.

He leans back in his chair and puts his hands behind his head. "I'm basking in the adoration of my peers."

"Well, I can see that." I pop open the top of my fizzy water and take a drink of it. All around us, people try to look as though they aren't watching us even though they clearly are.

"So, you going to ask?"

My eyebrows go up as I put my drink down. "Ask what?"

"If I did it." He tilts his head to the side, still parked in his cocky pose. "If I turned this third girl."

"Do you want me to?"

A rush of air escapes his lips as he shifts position, ending up leaning over the table toward me with his elbows on either side of his meal. His eyes search mine. "I can't tell if you're being trusting, or if you honestly don't care if I did it or not."

"Me neither," I admit. "But I think I'm being trusting."

He nods and picks up his fork. After several bites, he puts the utensil down again. "I didn't. I don't even know who she could be."

"Okay. I believe you." And I find I actually do.

"They didn't." He takes a deep breath. "Called in that freaky sorcerer chick again to cast a truth spell on me."

"Is it still in effect?"

He narrows his eyes at me. "I tell you the authorities violated my free will, and you want to know if you can do it, too?"

"Guess not. Or you would have answered that." I smile sweetly.

"I don't get you today."

"That makes two of us." I put my fork down. "I'm sorry. I'm just in a weird mood since..."

"Since you smelled the new all-were?"

I shake my head. "No. At least I don't think that was the trigger. I think it's because I've been as close to fighting with Simone as I ever have been."

"That why she's glaring at you?"

My hackles jump up. "What?"

Looking back to where we usually sit together, I see Simone sitting with Lyly. She isn't glaring at me though. Rather, she's pointedly ignoring me while Lyly glares at me.

"She's upset I'm talking to you, I guess."

"You were supposed to sit quietly alone and wait on her?"

"I usually do."

He laughs. "Until I showed up. That's me, disruptive influence and public menace."

"Yeah." I tap my fingers against the table. "Maybe I should go over and talk to her."

"She doesn't own you," he says.

I stare.

"What?" he asks.

"Nothing." I slouch in my chair. "That's just the second time someone has felt the need to remind me of that in the last hour. And he used those exact words."

"Think we might be onto something?"

"Maybe," I mumble. "But I don't think it's really like that. She's my best friend, you know?"

"Hey, I just got here." He spreads his hands wide before him. "I'll believe whatever you tell me. I won't even call in a spellcaster."

"You couldn't afford to call in a spellcaster." I grab my fork and scoop up a bite of food. "They've spent a lot of money on you."

"I wonder why..."

I swallow. "Just because doing the right thing is expensive, doesn't mean you shouldn't do it."

"I guess." He leans back, pressing his lips together as Michaela and Warren come into the room, together as they always seem to be these days. Michaela looks around, her gaze freezing on Troy for a heartbeat. Or maybe I imagine that... If so, Troy seems to be imagining it, too, based on the way he sits up and stares at her.

"She doesn't like seeing us together," Troy says.

"Really?" I focus my attention on Michaela again. She's turned away from us to say something to Warren, who watches her with total adoration. "You sure that's not wishful thinking?"

"Absolutely." He nods to where she's continuing to ignore us while Warren says something back. "See how studiously she's not looking over here? She wouldn't do that if it didn't bother her."

"I don't know... I think maybe she's just not looking this way." Her posture seems relaxed, and she's clearly having a conversation with someone on the other side of her.

"Trust me," he says.

I still don't believe him, but I shrug it off and concentrate on my food.

"I bet..." he says slowly, leaning back in his chair again. "I bet it would drive her crazy if she thought we weren't just friends."

Rolling my eyes seems like an inadequate response, so I add in, "I hate to break it to you, but I think she's happy with Warren."

"Then let's test it."

"Test it?" I give him a stare that I hope conveys I think he's insane. "I'm not dating you. You're completely hung up on your ex."

"You don't have to." His eyes are sparkling as he grins at me. "Just go to the equinox party with me."

"I don't know..."

"It'll be as friends," he says quickly. "But Mike won't know that. One slow dance and she'll go nuts."

The way my face crinkles up should tell him I'm skeptical, but I also put the sentiment in words. "I'd be willing to bet she won't."

"Bet what?"

I feel my eyes rolls again. "It's a figure of speech. You don't have anything to bet with."

"I'll do your homework for a week."

"That's unethical!" I answer without even pausing to consider it.

"Fine." Now it's his eyes that roll. "You win, and I'll do one thing you want me to. Anything."

"And if I'm wrong?"

He grins. "You kiss me."

I feel my forehead crunch up. "Why? I mean, if I'm wrong, don't you get back together with Michaela?"

"Sure. After you kiss me."

Laughing seems preferable to taking offense, so I do that. "Alright," I say. "You're on."

Too bad I didn't take him up on the homework offer. I could use a week off.

Chapter Nine

Tuesday seems nearly normal. The school doesn't put us on lockdown, but allows the usual Tuesday ski trip, and I spend it with Simone. It's odd because we're used to Amber being with us, and she isn't. But it's also routine because we do the same slopes we usually do, in the same order.

Humdrum same-as-always is broken when we get to the cafe after skiing, though. This is the point when we usually meet up with Seth and have coffee. Instead, we walk in and find him at a table with Amber, Raja, and Sam. Despite what he said yesterday, he's looking really close to the vixen at his side. As I watch, he takes a bite of the pastry on her plate. This action, predictably, fails to please Simone.

She trembles beside me. "We are still engaged."

My hand wraps around her arm, trying to keep her from storming over. "They're just friends, Simone. That's all."

Her head snaps to me. "You can look at that and think they're just friends?"

"He said-" I cut off, realizing my mistake.

The words have been spoken though and Simone latches onto their meaning instantly. She twists her arm out of my grasp. "When did you talk to him?"

I swallow and try not to look too guilty. "Yesterday. He came into the gym while I was working out."

"And you didn't tell me because...?" The full power of my friend's glower is now turned out me.

"I forgot? I mean, until I saw him just now." There is no way she's going to buy that.

Her eyes narrow.

"He just wanted to use the treadmill."

The snow outside is warmer than the look in Simone's eyes. "Yet you were talking."

"Well, he talked to me. It would be rude not-"

"Rude?" she yells. She pulls up to her full height, and there's no doubt that if she were in cat-form, her tail would be fully bristled. "And doing things behind my back? Is that not rude?"

As I try not to cry, I see Seth rise quickly and start toward us. I'm sure he means to help, but him getting involved is only going to make the scene uglier. I try to grab Simone's hand, but she yanks it away from me. "Please? Let's just get out of here, and we can talk."

"We can talk here." She plants her feet solidly on the floor and folds her arms in a classic stubborn stance. "Back-stabbers don't get to pick the venue they're confronted in."

"We were just talking," I lie quietly. My voice shakes like anything, but hopefully the tears in my eyes will make her think I'm just emotional.

"But you didn't tell me," she points out. "Which means you knew you were doing something wrong."

"I never meant to hurt you," I whisper, the words drowned out by Seth, who arrives with the declaration, "It's not her fault. I made her do it."

Simone's eyes narrow so tight that I'm not sure how she's seeing. "Made her do what, Seth?"

"Um..." He looks to me, clearly confused by the question.

"Talk to him," I answer. "But he didn't make me do it. He's just being an idiot. And should go mind his own business."

He pauses at that, and his features scrunch in what might be mild pain. "I think that if people are yelling about me in front of everyone I know, that's my business."

"What don't you want him saying?" Simone asks, knowing me all too well. "What did you two do?"

It's a direct question. One I can only answer with a half-truth. "We talked. I already admitted that."

73

Seth goes still as he realizes he's made the mess bigger than it was. "This is over talking to me?"

Simone's eyes swivel to him. "What did you think it was about?"

"She's not allowed to talk to me? Honestly? You've got to be kidding."

"Why would you be talking to her?" Simone demands. "And what else did you do, since you didn't think that's what I was upset about?"

The questions don't rattle him. "Trying to control who she talks to is abusive, Simone. And acting like she's not worth talking to is just plain mean. You're talking about the only one I know who believes you're a decent person."

I expect Simone to blow up at that, but she doesn't. Rather, she stands there looking like he just punched her in the gut. Slowly, she turns to me. Her voice is so quiet I can hardly hear it, even though no one else in the cafe is making a sound. "Just tell me what you did."

Seth shifts around Simone to stand beside me. "She isn't accountable to you. You don't own her."

Her gaze flickers to him, but then locks back on me. "Please?"

My chest aches. "I've been helping him learn self defense."

She takes a trembling breath. "So he can fight my father. You're helping him break my heart."

"No..." Tears flow freely down my cheeks now. I'm not sure when they started. "I just don't want to see him hurt. And I want you to be loved. He doesn't love you."

"Oh, he's made that abundantly clear." She shakes her head as she takes a backward step toward the door. "I thought you did though."

I start after her as she heads out the door, but then stop myself. She's not in any state to listen to me. My best hope it's to let her calm down, sulk, and sleep. In the morning, she'll want things to go back to normal and it will be easier to apologize.

Amber swoops in from the side and wraps her arms around me. As I rest my head against her shoulder, I realize how much I've missed her lately. I cling, astonished to note my tears dry up almost immediately.

"Come on." Seth puts his hand on my shoulder. "Sit down. I'll get you a drink. Hot chocolate?"

I pull back from Amber and nod. "Please."

As I follow my friend back to her table, I wipe my palms against my cheeks and smear the tears out. I must look a mess. Glancing at my hands shows a coating of eyeliner. Great. I don't know why Simone thinks we should be wearing makeup while skiing in the first place.

"Hey!" Raja yells as I sit down. "Don't you people have anything else to do?" She glares around the room as people slowly start to look away and resume their conversations.

Sam hands me a stack of napkins with a gentle smile. She's a petite redhead, one of the shortest people in our school, but she somehow seems large to me right now. Must be an effect of how small I feel.

"Thanks." I apply them to my streaked face, hoping that I'm helping rather than just making myself uglier.

"At least it's out in the open now?" Sam says, her voice gentle and her expression sincere.

Amber nods her agreement. "You can't move past secrets when they remain secrets."

"Should I have told her from the start?"

My fellow were-leopard winces. "No. Or maybe yes. I don't think there was any method of alleviating her anger."

"So I just shouldn't have done it."

My companions trade glances. It's Raja who speaks. "You could look at it that way. Or you could trust yourself to know what's right. You had good intentions, and if she can't accept that, maybe she's not a great friend."

"I really hurt her." I close my eyes, picturing her expression. "Did you see how she looked at me? It was like I'd killed her."

"What would you do if things were the other way around?" Raja asks. "Would you forgive her?"

Someone pats my hands where they're clasped on the table. I open my eyes to see it was Amber. She gives me a sad smile. "You'd forgive her anything, right?"

Sam looks like she's biting her tongue on something, so I direct my gaze to her. "Go on. Say it."

She shakes her head, but then goes for it. "You've forgiven her for being a bitch to you and everyone around you every day since you met her, haven't you?"

"She's not like that," I say, without as much conviction as I'd like.

"She wasn't," Amber says. "Not when we were younger. But this last year, she's really been struggling. Did you know she bellowed at me for wooing Raja? Called us dykes and everything."

"She didn't." But even as I deny the words, I know they're true. Amber doesn't lie.

"Afraid she did," Raja tells me. "I was there. Nearly punched her."

"Maybe you should have," Sam mutters. "What kind of friend says things like that?"

"Ones who hate change." Amber spreads her hands out in front of her. "Last year, she was upset to suddenly be here. This year she's upset her sister graduated. And now Seth's abandoning her, I'm procuring my own life, and even reliable old Rina is showing a spine. She's just not handling it well."

"And Rina's the one in therapy?" Sam asks. Then she flushes in embarrassment. "Sorry. I just know you go into Becky's office a lot. Maybe you volunteer there? It's not like you're sick every time you're with Nurse Sakura."

"No," I admit. "It's therapy. And, yeah, Simone could probably use some, too."

We fall silent as Seth arrives with my mug of cocoa. It's thick and smooth, just like always. But it doesn't warm my spirit the way it usually does.

Simone isn't on the bus home, and if she's in her room when I knock on the door, she doesn't let me know. It doesn't really worry me until she fails to show up for dinner though. I sit alone, looking for her every time someone walks into the room, until Seth gets tired of watching me from across the room and comes over.

"You being here won't help," I point out, my eyes on the door.

He sits down anyway. "She's trying to punish you. And you're letting her."

"Maybe I deserve to be punished."

"If you say so," he says. But he doesn't go anywhere, just sits there regarding me with those too-blue eyes of his. "Can I ask a possibly weird and definitely invasive question?"

"I reserve the right not to answer it, but sure."

He watches me for another moment. "Are you in love with Simone?"

I put my fork down, ever so gently. "Why do people keep thinking that? We're like sisters."

"Sorry." His gaze drops to the table. "Since Amber came out, I guess I've been seeing things."

"You didn't know about that, huh?" I fold my arms and lean back in my seat. "And it surprised you?"

He raises his eyebrows as he nods. "And made me realize how self-absorbed I must be. I thought I knew everything about her, but that was a pretty big thing to miss."

"I guess."

His eyes come up to mine, narrowing as they do. "Didn't surprise you though, did it? Which means she told you, but not me."

"Well..." I am very aware of being bright red at this moment. I shift awkwardly on my seat. "She didn't so much tell me as... um... let me know in another way."

He stares without blinking for a second, then his entire body relaxes. "So you do like girls. Good."

"Good?" Why on earth would that be good? "It's clearly not bad, but why is it good?"

"Oh..." He tilts his head as he thinks of his answer. "I guess I was just worried about you. You know, and that Troy guy."

That's the best answer he could come up with? "Simone's already told me I'm not allowed to be interested in him."

"That's not what I meant."

"Really?" I unfold my arms and put my hands on the edges of my tray. "Then what did you mean?"

"I'm just relieved you're only friends. That's all. Because I don't trust him." He thumps his palm against his head. "And I'm too stupid to keep my mouth shut. Forget I said it? Please."

Letting out my breath, I draw myself to my feet. "Sure," I say. But I leave without saying anything else, and it's not until I'm nearly to my room that I realize I left him with the impression I'm a lesbian. Oh, well. There are worse things he could think.

I open the door to my room, walk in, and shriek in surprise when I turn on the light and realize I'm not alone.

Simone turns away from the window and gives me a frosty glare. She holds her hand up in front of her face in a "stop!" kind of way. "Don't say anything. I didn't come here to talk to you."

Um... but she is talking to me... not that I'm stupid enough to point that out.

"You betrayed me, Katerina. You were the last person I thought would ever do that."

"I just-"

"Don't!" she cuts me off with a scream. "I'm not going to listen to it. I only came here to tell you I don't ever want to talk to you again."

The claim lands like a series of punches.

"And," she goes on, spitting out the words, "I wanted to apologize to you. For all the years when I made you think you're better than you are. Because I should have told you the truth. I should have made you see how far below me -- how far below everyone -- you are. There's a reason your parents didn't want to keep you."

Whoa. I stare in shock for moment. My eyes sting, and assorted emotions vie for dominance. Anger wins, and makes me bellow, "And I should have let you know you're a complete bitch!"

"I see," she says, her voice as warm as the tundra. "That's what pretending you were worth something got us, you thinking you can judge me. You can't. Because you're not my equal, you never were. And you're certainly not my friend."

As I stand trembling, she stalks to the door and throws it open. I summon enough willpower to say, "I was. But you weren't ever mine, were you?"

She tosses out one last sentence, "I could never be friends with someone not worthy of my respect."

And the door slams shut.

Chapter Ten

I resist the urge to write either my mother or my fostermom. My mother's not so good with emotion, and Eileen should be kept out of this. I try to meditate, but it doesn't get me anywhere, so I stuff myself into gym clothes and go downstairs to set the treadmill on infinite mode.

Soon, I'm sweating enough to hide my tears. Or so I tell myself.

At some point, my world narrows down to my feet and the moving tread beneath them. I close my eyes and focus on feeling my muscles move. Time flutters and drifts by like falling snow. Until someone clears his throat.

Reluctantly, I open my eyes. Dots appear across my vision, but through them I see Troy watching me with a frown.

"You don't look so good, kitty-girl."

I'd say something back, but it would take more air than I have available.

"No, really." He steps closer. "You should stop. You're wavering like you're going to faint. Saw a guy do it at football practice once."

The spots of light dancing around him would probably agree.

"We don't have to talk about it. Or even think about it. You can just practice throwing me around. I hear you like doing that."

I shake my head, and a wave of dizziness slams into me. I grab the sides of the treadmill, and my feet jump to the sides. The treads pass between my legs as I gasp for oxygen.

Troy reaches around to turn the machine off, and I climb silently down. He's dressed in his usual attire: jeans and one of the three shirts he owns, the blue North Sky hoodie. Nevertheless, he goes and tosses some of the stacked mats onto the floor.

Two refills of my water bottle later, he kicks his shoes off and positions himself in a waiting stance. It's not perfect; his feet are a little too close together, and his hands aren't quite right, but it's good enough for me to learn he has some kind of training in his background. Interesting.

I remove my own shoes and go stand across from him. We bow and return the waiting stance.

The clock ticks.

At the same time, we move. His right foot lunges into a front stance while I shift into a back one. He moves his left foot into a kick that I catch easily. I use my hold to twist, flipping him to the ground.

He lets out a grunt as he lands. "That was fast."

"Try being less predictable," I advise.

After climbing back up, he goes again into a front stance, but this time he waits to see what I do. I send a punch toward the left shoulder, then use his distraction to sweep his right foot out from under him, and he hits the mat again.

"That might not be your best stance," I tell him. "It would work alright if I were slower, but I'm not human like the other people you've sparred with."

"But you can tell I've sparred with someone?" He leans back on his elbows, his legs crossing at his feet as he looks up sheepishly. "I'm that competent at least?"

I chuckle. "Yeah. You've studied something. Tae Kwon Do would be my guess. Your form needs work, but mostly you need to be more aware of your opponent."

"Or maybe I need an easier opponent." He gets up again and goes into the waiting pose.

"You should come to hengedo. We meet on Sundays."

The smile he gives me doesn't have much humor in it. "I don't think that's a good idea. I'm not exactly the most popular person in this school."

"So, what, you think people would team up on you?"

"You think they wouldn't?"

I toss a light kick against his ankle, just to get him moving. "I don't think so. And you'd have me and Penny to stand up for you if they did."

"Or you two could just tutor me..."

"I already have someone I'm tutoring." I bat back a jab of pain at the reminder of the fight. Then I start to wonder... I was thinking I needed another student for Seth to spar with rather than facing me all the time.

My opponent takes advantage of my distraction to land several rapid blows then sweep my feet from under me. I latch onto him, pulling him down with me. I flip over as we land, so that I have him pinned under me. "That was not a legal move sequence."

He grins unapologetically. "But it got the pretty girl on top of me, didn't it?"

I smack the side of his head and roll off him, but I'm laughing as I do it. I stare up at the ceiling as I catch my breath. "Thank you. For coming to check on me."

"Yeah, well, I was kind of told to."

Told to? "By whom?"

"That snow leopard guy." He rolls onto his side and props his head up so that he's looking down at me. "He was worried, but said you were mad at him for something."

"Was I? I don't even remember." I let out a breath. "Weird that he went to you. Have you two ever talked before?"

"Nope. Didn't talk much this time."

I turn my head to study Troy's face. His expression is impossible to read, but there's something in it that makes my chest feel tight. "Would you like to?"

He looks at me funny.

"I'm tutoring him in this stuff. You could join his classes. I think it would be good for both of you."

"I don't know…"

"Come on. I'm not asking you to be best buds, just to enter a series of civil bouts with the guy."

He laughs. "Because you're still mad at him?"

"I'm not mad at him anymore." I shake my head, then regret it as it brings a stabbing pain to my temples and little dancing lights to my vision. "I don't have the energy."

He smiles. "You don't look like you have the energy to make it back to your room. You going to sleep here?"

"It's tempting." But I drag myself to a sitting position. The world wobbles. Yeah, I need to get to bed.

"I'll clean up," Troy offers, getting to his feet before holding down a hand to help me up.

I sway as I stand. "Thanks for that, too, then."

I stumble up the stairs, passing a few people who shy away from me either because I'm a pariah or because I smell. Probably both. Because not only am I an outcast, I'm a stinky one.

Without bothering to turn on the light, I stagger to bed and collapse on top of the sheets. Sleep arrives almost instantly.

I float through Wednesday on a cloud of numbness, avoiding people whenever possible. I skip breakfast, not in the least bit hungry, and grab a lunch from the student kitchen, which I eat in the sickbay as I help Nurse Sakura weed expired bottles from her storage cabinet and reorganize the remaining meds. I'm in my room forgoing dinner in favor of meditation when someone knocks on the door. I ignore it at first, but when they knock again, I pull myself back to the world and answer.

It's Amber, alone for once, and scowling. "You need to eat."

"I ate lunch."

She raises an eyebrow. "A granola bar?"

I consider trying to lie, but nod anyway.

"That is not adequate sustenance." She reaches into the room, grabs my arm, and pulls me forward. "You're coming to dinner."

Amber is much less controlling than Simone, but when she gets it into her mind that you're going to do something, it's a lot easier to go along with it than to fight. So I go with her, trudging down the hall in my fuzzy Hello Kitty slippers.

She takes me to the counter for food, but doesn't get anything herself because she says she already ate. In fact, most of the school has already eaten, and the kitchen staff has already started cleaning up, although they seem happy enough to make me a plate anyway.

"There you go, sweetie." The matron of the kitchen, a plump polar bear named Ms. Gallahan, hands me two things. One, a plate of pot roast and sides, and the other a huge bowl of butterscotch pudding. "And I believe that's your favorite."

"Yeah..." I stare at the bowl for a moment, tears pricking at my eyes. I can't believe she knows that. I make myself look up and meet her gaze. "Thank you, Ms. Gallahan."

She smiles softly, nods to me, and returns to the sink full of dishes in the back. One of the other workers winks at me from where he stands organizing silverware. I'm not sure what to make of that, but give him a weak smile and take my food to a table near the windows.

Outside, snow falls lackadaisically, the flakes drifting slowly through the night. It's possibly our last snowfall of the year.... I stare at it until Amber pokes me in the arm and says, "Eat."

Dutifully, I take a bite. I'm pretty sure it's good, but I can hardly taste it.

Amber motions me to eat more. "I know you're hurting, kitten, but you need to take care of yourself."

She gets up, returning a minute later with a teapot and two cups. "Chamomile," she says. "For calming the nerves."

I thought it was supposed to put you to sleep, but as I wouldn't mind passing out, I don't object to drinking it when she pours me some. It's sweet and comforting in its warmth.

"I'm sorry," Amber says.

I squint at her as she spins her teacup in a slow circle in front of her. "What did you do?"

"I haven't been there for you." She gives me a quiet but sincere look. "I've been so wrapped up in Raja that I didn't even realize the situation I'd left you in. I've been a really inferior friend of late."

While there's some amount of truth in what she's saying, I can't let her beat herself up for being happy. "No, you haven't. You've made time for me every time I've asked you to."

"Well, I should be making more." She nods emphatically. "And I'm going to."

"It'll upset Simone."

The noise she makes is probably the rudest one that's ever come out of her. "I can't believe you're still concerned over her. She told me what she said to you. Or the synopsis of it, I should say."

"Oh." I stare at the food still on my plate. I don't really want to finish it. "Did she tell you what I said to her?"

"She did." Amber grins around a sip of tea. "And I told her I couldn't agree with you more."

"You did?" I ask, the question nearly a whisper.

"Of course." She puts her cup down carefully and leans over to push my hair back from my face. "She had no right to speak to you like that. You have more worthiness in your pinky toe than she has anywhere."

I shake my head as tears shed from my eyes. "Don't be mean to her. She was just hurt."

"She still shouldn't have said it." Amber relaxes against the back of her chair. "What she should be doing is thanking God she has you to stand up for her. Because we all know no one else is going to do it."

"She used to be your friend, too. Before high school at least. That was real, right?"

"Yeah, well, she's been a different person since she came here." Amber lets out a sigh. "I do miss who she used to be. But that's not her anymore. I don't know why, but it isn't. And

I can't handle dealing with this new her while hoping the old one will come back. Because she just keeps getting worse."

Much as I want to, I can't argue with her. Instead, I rearrange my tray, moving the half-eaten pot roast to the back to make room at the front for the pudding. I give the dessert a stir, bringing out the scent of butterscotch. Usually, that would make me hungry. Today it just stagnates in my nostrils.

It takes effort, but I make myself eat all of the pudding. Amber accepts this as a full meal and lets me leave after that, although she follows me to my room and insists on watching a movie with me. She doesn't even argue with me when the movie I pick out is black-and-white and doesn't star anyone still alive.

The next day is the second of our weekly on-snow days. I ride up across the aisle from Amber and Raja, but tell them to go do their own thing when we get there. "I'm going to practice snowboarding some more."

They leave me to it, but I go first to the slope-side equipment shop. There are cheaper places in town to buy equipment, but without a car they're hard to get to. Besides, when I talked to my father about this in email, he said it was fine for me to spend however much I wanted getting myself my own board and boots.

Since I'm not going to get anything unique here, I get something really simple with the plan to customize it later. The fastest they can get the bindings on is in an hour, so I spend the time outside building a snowman. This seems to amuse the people who pass me, judging by how they laugh and send out encouragements.

As I draw near completion, a shadow falls across my artwork, and I look behind me to see Seth knocking his helmet against his leg as he watches me. He wears a bemused expression that makes me want to go over and hug him. Or it would if I was willing to make Simone even more mad at me.

He sees me looking and straightens. His expression shifts through a couple of things, until it's eventually a careful form of neutral. "You okay?"

"Yeah. Just waiting for my board to be ready."

His brow creases with a cute little furrow. "Board?"

"Yeah. I'm being a new me," I say as I turn back to my snowman. He needs some gravel or buttons for eyes and a mouth, but all we have is snow.

"Good." He pauses. "Um... Not that the old you was bad. Just that it's good to see you doing what you want to do."

"Rather than what Simone wants me to do?" I bend to pick up some snow with the intent of making little balls for eyes. "I guess."

"Still, snowboarding seems a little extreme."

I glance over my shoulder to see a smile teasing his lips.

"Oh, it's just the beginning," I tell him. "Come spring, I'm taking up roller derby." He laughs at the idea, which maybe I should find insulting. "Hey, I can be tough."

"Oh, I know that." He grins at me. "I was just thinking that they'll never know what hit them."

My cheeks heat up as our eyes meet, and I see he meant what he just said. Quickly, I turn away and hope he didn't notice the blush.

"Why don't you use coins?" he asks.

I finish sticking on the eyeball I've created. It doesn't stand out very much. "Coins would be better. I don't have any though."

Warmth approaches my back as Seth draws near and reaches over my shoulder to place a penny in the place of the other eye. "How's that?"

"Much better." I'm not sure how I get the words out, as it's suddenly hard to breathe.

He reaches over the other shoulder and exchanges my snowy eye with another copper one before taking a step back.

I draw in a huge breath and try not to shiver.

"Kinda morbid though," he says.

"Morbid?" I frown at the face of my snowman and step back as well, going to the side to keep from getting too close again.

"They used to put coins on the eyes of the dead."

My frown turns to Seth. "Dude. You just killed my snowman."

His lips part as he struggles for a comeback. The look is too comical for me to keep up my straight face, and I have to laugh. A slow smile spreads on his face in answer. God, he's gorgeous...

"I have to go," I blurt. "Board should be ready."

"Okay..." he responds slowly. He looks like he might possibly have something else to say after that, but I don't hang around to hear it. I leave him standing there, the sun glittering on the white strands of his hair as the wind ruffles it.

What's wrong with me? It must be because the moon is so close to full. Seth is the last person I can let myself go gaga over. If Simone's mad at me now, imagine how irate she'd be if she had any idea what I was just thinking. Besides, there was a time when I was making out with his twin sister. So call that two good reasons to avoid him until I return to sanity.

And I will return to sanity. Quickly. Because if I'm going to be punished for helping him prepare for the Challenge, then I need to keep helping him.

Chapter Eleven

I start to snowboard by myself, but I'm spotted on my first run by a lift chair full of wolves who yell at me to wait for them at the bottom.

To my surprise, I actually do make it to the bottom before they catch up with me, but I'm not waiting long when Penny carves to a stop beside me. She leans over and gives me an awkward partial-hug. "Hey, girl! You doing alright?"

"Still going too slow, but I'm getting better."

She gives me a bit of a look, but accepts the answer without saying anything, even though I know full well that wasn't what she meant.

Madison rides up next, the hair sticking out from under her snowy white helmet a bright green today. She gestures down at my new board, which is very obviously not a rental. "So, you've finally admitted you're one of us now?"

"Something like that. I'm trying this new thing where I do what I feel like doing, rather than what other people want me to be doing."

"You rebel!" Madison teases as Penny grins at me. "You feel like riding back up with us?"

Maria and Jonathan join us, and we head up in two groups, me between Madison and Penny. It occurs to me that someone is missing. "Where's Troy? The park?"

The others look at each other.

"What?"

Madison shakes her head. "It's okay, you've had your own drama to deal with. He's grounded for the duration."

"Until they figure out what's up with the new all-were," Penny adds.

A tide of guilt crushes over me that I had no idea he's been trapped in school since we smelled the new female. "He didn't tell me that."

"Well..." Madison shrugs. "Like I said, you've had your own drama. I hope it's settled?"

I wrap my hands around the edge of the seat, my gloves insulating me from the metal. "I'm not sure 'settled' is the right word."

"But you're off doing your own thing,'" she points out as a wind rushes down the slope and tries to freeze us. "So things must be better than yesterday, because you were just hiding yesterday."

"I guess." The chair jerks slightly as we pass by lift tower nine. For some reason it always does that just there. "But there's more coming. Whether she forgives me or not, there's going to be something else."

"She forgives you?" Penny asked. "What about whether or not you forgive her?"

"Penny!" Madison chides.

I shake my head. "No, it's alright. She has a point. Simone's hurt me, too."

Penny snorts. "She's abused you for years."

"Penny!" Madison says again. "We've talked about this."

The younger wolf looks off to the left, toward Mount Denali, and makes no response as yet another gust of wind slams her coal-colored hair against her face.

"You've talked about me being abused?" I aim the question at Madison, even though Penny is the talkative one.

The senior lets out a long breath. "This isn't the time to talk about it. But, yeah, there's some concern that you're in an abusive relationship."

I want to laugh, but I can't quite manage it. I make a garbled choking sound instead, and probably sound like I'm insane. Or dying. Dying from insanity, maybe. "At least you're not trying to tell me I'm in love with her."

Madison's eyebrows draw together. "Who said that?"

"A few people."

"Boys, I bet." She chuckles. "They just can't tell the difference between a girl friend and a girlfriend, can they?"

I laugh too. "That's one way of putting it."

"I bet Seth was one of them. Does he have any female friends he hasn't tried to get too close to?"

My laughter becomes a distant memory. "What do you mean?"

"She means," Penny says, rejoining the conversation, "that we caught him up to something with that fox girl. And we all know that before Warren put a stop to it, he had a thing going on with Mike."

"Up to what?" I hear myself ask, even though I would never intentionally do such a thing. "I mean, he told me they were just friends."

The wolves both look away and act like they're preparing to get off the chair, even though it's a tower too early for that.

"Guys?"

Predictably, Penny's the one who breaks. "They were totally making out."

Oh. "When?"

"Saturday."

So, after he told me there was nothing up between them. Something must have changed. "So, maybe they're going out now?" I'd be lying if I claimed I feel nothing as I speculate, but I'm not willing to look at what I feel.

"If so, they suck at it."

The gossip pauses while we slide off the unloading ramp and go sit at the head of one of the trails down. Penny leans close so the other won't hear her. "Saw them today. Sam was totally holding hands with Bryce, and Seth was right there."

Which means that either Seth and Samantha are polyamorous, or, more likely, they're not dating. Unless they are dating, but are doing it behind Bryce's back... But I don't think either of them would do that. Not that I really know Samantha Fox all that well...

I shove the speculation out of my head and focus on riding the snow. The shift succeeds, and we're on the bus home before I think about Seth again, and then it's only because he slides into the seat next to me with a cheerful hello.

"How was boarding?" he asks, seemingly oblivious to the fact that Penny and Madison, in the seat behind ours, had been talking to me before he showed up.

Sitting crooked in the seat as I am means that his thigh is now dangerously close to my shin. I do my best to ignore that detail and grunt, "Fine."

"Good." He leans back in the seat, making himself quite at home there, and turns his neck so he can see me. "You taken the board into the park yet?"

"No."

We stare at each other for a moment. I know the blue in his eyes is a serious flaw, but I can't help marveling at exactly how close it is to the color of the sky.

He turns his shoulder into the seat to see me better. "Am I bothering you? Do you want me to leave?"

Conflicting answers bounce around my head. I can't take too long to answer, or he'll take that as me telling him to go. And I find myself not wanting to do that to him. "No, you're fine. I'm just tired."

Penny leans over the seat back. "Tired and busted."

Busted? Seth and I both squint at her, then look to where she points. My stomach plummets as I behold Simone and Lyly standing at the front of the bus with equally pissed-off looks.

"You may as well stay," Penny goes on as I flinch under the weight of Simone's glower. "Looks like the damage has been done."

"We're not doing anything," Seth points out.

I don't look at him as I answer. "We're sitting together."

"So?"

Penny snorts as Simone breaks eye contact with me to sit huffily in the front row. "So Rina's probably not supposed to talk to you, let alone sit inches from you. What part of you being Simone's property confuses you?"

He turns slowly, twisting far enough to stare at the wolf. "The part where it reflects reality."

She shrugs at him. "It's reality for her."

"And you?" he asks, turning to me.

"Not exactly."

His eyebrows go up as a look of incredulity takes over his features.

"I mean, obviously she doesn't actually own you," I start. His expression softens a little. "But if you belonged to anyone, it would be her."

"And I have no say in this?"

I fumble for words.

"You can't think that," he says. "If you thought that, you wouldn't be helping me train."

Thankful for the respite, I nod with enthusiasm. "Right."

"But the other day she did yell at you just for talking to me, so you're really not supposed to?"

"Well..." I swallow awkwardly. "Not alone anyway. You know, without Simone."

He stares at me. "I always thought you didn't like me. I've been trying to figure out what changed your mind."

"Why wouldn't I like you?"

"I don't know. It made more sense than you not being allowed to acknowledge my existence. Exactly how controlling is Simone?" He holds up a hand. "Never mind. Question retracted. I know the answer, and you'd just make an excuse about it."

"Excuse?"

"Yeah," Penny chimes in. "You'd say something about how it isn't that you don't have permission to talk to whoever you want to, it's just that you don't want to hurt Simone."

"Exactly." Seth nods to her, then moves his eyes back to me. "That's what you were going to say, right?"

It was, but I'd feel stupid admitting it, so I just shrug.

Penny props her chin on the back of my seat, putting her face halfway between me and Seth. "I think that if you're going to make her mad, you should make her really mad. Do something to deserve it."

"Like what?" I ask dismissively. "Ravish each other in the aisle?"

Seth makes a choked sort of sound.

Penny's eyes narrow. "I was thinking more along the line of going to the dance next week."

I shake my head. "For one thing, that would be needlessly antagonizing Simone. She's mad at me, but I don't hate her. Second, I already told Troy I'd go with him."

"Troy?" Seth asks. "Does he-"

"As friends," I say quickly, before he can out me to the wolves. "He's thinking it has a chance of making Michaela jealous."

"It doesn't," Penny and Seth chorus.

"I know. And I told him that."

"Well, then," say Penny, turning her head to face Seth. "Guess you'll have to go with me."

Chapter Twelve

When we get back, there's a sign on the door telling us that we're not to leave the building tonight. I assume it has something to do with the new all-were. It doesn't really bother me, because I wasn't planning to go out anyway. I take my usual indoor run and a shower, then head to dinner. I'm on my way to the counter to get my food when Troy grabs my arm. "I've got something you have to see."

His words contradict his actions as he drags me across the dining room rather than showing me the sheaf of papers clutched in his other hand. I crane my neck to see the printouts, but can't get a good enough look to read them.

We zoom straight for the table where Michaela sits. She looks up from a glass of chocolate milk and squints in apprehension. Beside her, Warren stiffens. Michaela lowers her glass and moves her hand to her boyfriend's leg. He relaxes ever so slightly, but still doesn't look happy to see us.

Without preamble, Troy shoves the papers toward his ex. She raises her eyebrows at them as Warren leans in to read the top page.

"Skinwalkers?" the wolf asks.

"It explains us!" Troy may be answering Warren's question, but his eyes are locked on Michaela. "The weres have never heard of anything like us because we're not weres. We're skinwalkers!"

Michaela takes the papers from Troy, and frowns at them. "What's a skinwalker?"

"It's a myth," says Warren. "And you can't be skinwalkers because they don't exist."

Michaela's eyes flick to him, and she gives him a fond little smile. "Neither do werewolves."

"Besides..." Warren takes the papers and flicks to the second one. He jabs his finger at a section. "See here? Skinwalkers can only change into something if they're wearing its pelt."

We all look at him. He found that awfully fast...

Michaela sighs. "You've researched this already, haven't you?"

"Researched every possible explanation for my life mate having the powers she has?" Warren poses before offering the papers back to Troy, his eyes not leaving Michaela's. "Yes, I have."

Troy folds his arms, refusing to take the printouts. "And it never occurred to you some of the details could be wrong?"

"Some of the details?" Warren flips to another section and reads from it, "'To achieve these supernatural powers, the skinwalker must first murder a close blood relative, engage in incest, or commit necrophilia.' Mike hasn't done any of that, but have you?"

He's answered with a glare from Troy and an unexpected input from across the table. Lyly's sister Aliah makes a dismissive sound. "In some stories, werewolves are cursed the same way. He may have a point."

"You think so?" Michaela asks her friend as she takes the papers from Warren and looks over the one he's currently turned to.

"Maybe?" Aliah pushes a chunk of pure white hair behind her ear, which is nearly as pale. Her bright red eyes are thoughtful. "I mean, you can only turn into things you know, right? Maybe the thing with the pelt is just a way of saying you have to know what the creature looks like?"

"Exactly!" Troy exclaims, beaming at the albino and spreading his arms out wide.

"Okay," says Warren as he leans back and folds his arms. "So why aren't there more of you?"

"Who says there aren't?" Troy counters. "Not to beat a dead horse, but I didn't know any werewolves back in Seattle. Did you, Mike?"

"I wouldn't have known they were werewolves if I did," she answers slowly. "I knew foxes without knowing it."

"Right!" He moves to her side, takes her shoulders, and turns her to face him. "There could be a whole secret community of us somewhere."

A low rumble comes from Warren, who glares at Troy and his hands. It gets louder until even Troy notices the growl and lets go of Michaela. She reaches behind her to pat Warren's knee and he grabs her hand in both of his.

"Just think about it," Troy says. Then he heads out of the room, leaving me caught between staying and going. I hesitate for a moment, then hurry after him. He turns at the entrance to the room and heads in the direction of the library.

Since most of us have our own computers, there are only two somewhat antique models in the library. I expect him to go to one of them, but instead he targets the catalog machine. He walks up to it and types something in, bringing up the "I'm thinking!" spinning clock on the screen.

"You think we have a book on skinwalkers?"

"No." He drums his fingers on the desk as the search continues. The catalog computer is about a million years old, so it can take some time to spit out results. "I already tried that. I'm thinking Navaho legends might have a hit, though."

"I think you'd be better off on the Internet."

He shakes his head. "I just keep seeing the same information over and over on the Internet."

The computer finishes its search and happily lets us know there were no hits. "You could try Native American myths, but I'd be surprised if you found anything."

I pull out my phone and run a quick search on Amazon, but all they have for "skinwalker" is a bunch of romance novels. A few of them look decent, but they're probably not going to help any.

The catalog reports a list of three books for "Native American myth," but all of the natives in question are from Alaska, not the lower forty-eight. The library aide, Aniu, appears and tries to help, but all she comes up with that we hadn't found already is a few paragraphs in someone's biography. And the biography is very clear that the person involved did not like skinwalkers, as he apparently found them evil.

"This is pointless," Troy grumbles as soon as Aniu is gone. "What I need to do is go find that other skinwalker out there."

Chill bumps shiver down my arms. "Are you sure that's safe?"

He snorts. "It's safe unless the other weres find out. They'll kick me out of here if I leave the building, and being here is the only reason your friendly elders didn't murder me."

"Maybe she'll come here?" I propose.

His eyes scrunch as he considers this. "Possible, if she's here because she's following my scent. But what if she was just passing through? And what if to her, smelling a skinwalker is normal? What if she'd never imagine I'd be desperate to meet another one? She could have smelled me and walked right along."

"I'm sure people are looking for her. Mr. Atherton would have told the Council."

"Oh, that's reassuring. This is the same council that murdered Kim."

I don't really want to rehash the Kim debate. He's never going to see her execution as lawful. "They're not going to kill this new all-were unless she does something atrocious. They don't kill unprovoked."

"It just doesn't take much to provoke them?" He jams his hands into his pockets and stares toward the window. It's too dark for us to see anything other than the reflection of indoor lights. "What if she doesn't know their rules any more than Kim did?"

I stare at the glass reflection of me. She could be out there scared, alone, and in desperate need of a friend, just like Troy had been. On the other hand, she could be sitting on the other side of the courtyard, just inside the protection of the trees as she plots who knows what.

"Tomorrow's the first night of the moon," I say. "They'll have to let us outside for that. I'll sniff around in cat-form."

Troy smiles at me. "You're the best."

"I know." I just hope it doesn't get me killed.

Chapter Thirteen

The ball of anxiety in my stomach when I wake doesn't dissipate as I go through the day, and by sunset I'm an anxious wreck. I struggle not to let on about this, but my scent has to be broadcasting it far and wide.

We drift outdoors in the minutes before moonrise, each species going to the section of grounds we usually shift in. Simone stands yards from the rest of us snow leopards and glares out toward the trees.

Seth slides up to me. "Why are you nervous?"

I briefly consider lying about it, either by claiming not to be nervous or by giving him a fake story about why, but in the end I don't. "I promised Troy I'd sniff around for him."

"No."

His sister swats at him. "You don't own her. She can sniff if she wants to."

Seth narrows his eyes at Amber. "She's going to go looking for the other all-were."

"Oh." Amber looks stunned for a moment, but recovers quickly. "Then we'll journey and sniff with her. Safety can be found in numbers, you know."

The Dae twins continue to look at each other, Seth not seeming pleased and Amber pretending not to notice as she stretches her muscles as though loosening up for a race.

The first tingles of the moon just beginning to crest the horizon zip through my body. The familiar exhilaration of allowing my wild inner-leopard to surface embraces me, and I laugh. Then, between one heartbeat and the next, I shift into my cat-form, my paws sinking ever so slightly into the snow and my tail lashing merrily.

Amber continues to stretch. Her back arches up and she kneads at the ground with her claws before she straightens out. Her eyes go to the trees, and she cocks her head as though asking, "Shall we?"

Seth's tail twitches unhappily. He clearly doesn't think it's a good idea. I'm not sure he isn't right, but I nod to his sister anyway, and we trot out.

When we pass Simone, she huffs at us, turns her back, and sits down like a house cat pretending to ignore her human. It breaks my heart a little, but there's nothing I can do about it.

We head off to the area the new all-were was originally smelled in, taking a long arc around the wolves' territory. Forgetting for a few moments that there could be danger involved, I let myself revel in the details of running: the whisper of wind through my fur, the warm stretching of muscles, and the icy bite of the snow on my paws.

The scent is long gone, of course, so I have to tell the others where to stop by rushing in front of them and coming to a halt. We walk slowly around the clearing, smelling nothing more interesting than some rabbits. Seth jerks his head back toward the school after that, but Amber and I insist on another, wider circle.

It's on the third lap that Amber stiffens with her nose pointed south. I can't smell whatever she's caught, and from the way Seth is sniffing he can't either. Nevertheless, we follow her as she veers off the circular path.

Yards pass before my nose latches onto the all-were scent. It's incredibly faint, but it grows stronger as we continue. It's subtly different from the others I've smelled, telling me it's not just Michaela doing the same thing we're doing.

My ears pick up a quiet rustle after close to an hour of being on the scent. It's in this instant that I realize I have absolutely no idea what we're supposed to do should we actually find our target. Hopefully, she'll be friendly. Because if she isn't, I have no idea how to fight her.

With the moon full, we shouldn't come across anyone in human form out here, but a distinctly human shape appears before us. I startle. How did she get so close so quietly and without me noticing?

The all-were is younger than I expected, about my age, as far as I can tell in the dim lighting. She has pale brown skin, dark eyes, and long brunette hair. "You're not native here," she says.

I sit and look at her. I wish I had a way to speak, but I don't have enough control over my change yet to shift back into human form before the moon sets. I thought neither of the twins could either, but Seth surprises me by speaking. "Neither are you."

"Touché." She takes a step closer, her head cocked to the side. "Are you werewolves? You don't smell like wolves."

"We're snow leopards," Seth answers. His voice sounds strained, probably from the effort of staying in human form. "Are you a skinwalker?"

Her eyes narrow. "A what? I don't think so. I'm-"

She cuts off and her head snaps to the side like she heard something we didn't.

"I have to go," she says.

Then, before we can object, she's sprouted wings and feathers. She squawks apologetically and launches herself into the air. She's gone in a heartbeat. Whatever kind of bird she just became is a really fast one.

I sniff the air in the direction she looked before she fled. I don't smell whatever it was that spooked her.

Teeth snap in my face.

Seth, back in cat-form, moves in front of me, blocking me from investigating further. Instinctively, my lips curl back into a snarl.

His paw comes out of nowhere to smack against my head. *Ouch!*

As I stare at him, his nose drops and he looks ashamed of himself for the show of dominance. He steps aside, giving me the option of trying to find the source of the all-were's distress.

Amber takes a few step toward home, turns, and looks at us in question. Seth starts after her immediately, but I take a second to think about it.

Whatever else is out here, the all-were who spoke to us was clearly afraid of it. Do I really want to track down something that can scare someone who can turn into any beast she can imagine? I kinda think I don't. Certainly not alone.

I follow the twins and arrive back at the school with plenty of time to spare. We rest for a good long while, then Seth stretches and ambles over to me. He bends his front legs and lowers his head. It takes me a moment to realize he's bowing. He's inviting me to fight with him.

It makes sense that he should practice combat in cat-form as well as in human. And I suppose it's fair to give him a chance to kick my ass, considering the number of times I've tossed him on his. Of course, I'm assuming he has training in this that's at least equal to mine. If I'm better trained, I may have a shot. But if we're on par with one another, then his size should be the determining factor.

I wait for him to make the first move, then dodge the swipe of his paw when he does. I let him back me up several feet, then pounce forward. The move manages to take him by surprise, and we tumble into the snow.

I get a quick nip at his neck, but his mass allows him to flip me off easily. We roll and he ends up on top. My hind paws are against his stomach, where they would be hurting him if I unsheathed my claws, but his jaws find my throat without me being able to stop them.

He backs off, breathing heavily.

After a short rest, we start again. And again. And again. I win one of the four little battles we have, and come close another two times before I'm too tired to keep it up anymore,.

We go to where Amber sleeps and lie down on each side of her, huddling together to better stay warm. I feel bad for Simone, alone across the clearing from us. But there's still nothing I can do about that, so I force myself not to think about her. It doesn't really work, because my dreams end up being of her, but at least I get to sleep.

I stay asleep until moonset hits and shifts me back to human-form, when being next to someone is no longer enough to keep me warm. If I were alone, it's possible I'd go back to sleep anyway and die of hypothermia, but Seth shakes me when I fail to get up and pesters me to my feet.

"Thanks," I mumble as he helps me keep my balance. He looks way too awake, all things considered.

"No problem." He smiles, his eyes on my hair. Reaching a hand up tells me why. It's a tangled mess up there. That's probably funny if it's not your hair. Seth's, on the other hand, looks like he just brushed it.

"Inside!" says Amber, rubbing her arms. "Cold!"

She rushes toward the building, and after checking to make sure Simone was up and moving I follow. Seth walks beside me, the clouds from our breaths mingling in the lamp light. Above us, the Aurora Borealis shines in a brilliant display of greens and blues.

Together, our footsteps slow down until we're stopped, looking up at the sky.

"I never get used to it," Seth says quietly.

"Yeah," I agree. "You'd think you would, but it's always magic, isn't it?"

We stand together watching the sky. It's worth shivering for.

But when I look down to find Simone standing a few feet away and glaring at me, I wonder if the experience of shared wonder was worth escalating her wrath.

Then she speaks, her words more like a series of growls than normal speech. "Get away from him, you slut."

Instinctively, I start to step away. But I'm stopped when Seth's hand lashes out and grabs my arm. He actually moves closer to me, drawing near enough for me to feel his heat cutting through the frigid air.

"She's not doing anything wrong," he says.

Simone's lip quivers as though she's about to cry. Despite her nastiness, it makes me want to hug her. "You don't care about me at all, do you? My feelings mean nothing to you."

Seth's hand falls away from me, somewhat guiltily unless I'm imagining things. "Simone..."

"Save it," she snaps. She even puts her hand up as though physically holding off any words he may utter. She stomps to the building, leaving us alone and cold. The northern lights still play overhead, but the magic is gone.

Chapter Fourteen

I go to bed intending to tell Troy about finding the other all-were as soon as I get up for the day, but by the time I'm awake and dressed I've convinced myself it's too dangerous. The female is afraid of something out there, so it stands to reason it's dangerous for him too. And I don't trust that fact to keep him from rushing out to search for himself.

To be sure my logic is sound, I go looking for one of the Dae twins. Seth I find in the music room, scribbling notations. His face is pale, and his eyes are puffy. I don't think he went to sleep after we came back in. Knowing him, he's been at the piano since then. The stack of papers sitting in front of him backs up the idea that he's been composing for some time now.

Not seeming to notice my entry, he plays a series of notes, then plays them again at a slightly different tempo. He nods to himself and writes something down. Placing his pencil between his teeth, he stares into the distance, obviously listening to sounds I can't hear.

I've always loved the moments I've stolen watching him write music. He's so enraptured, like he's talking to God, and God's talking back. There's nothing in my life I feel that way about, and I envy him more than a little.

Before I talk myself out of interrupting him, I knock lightly on the door frame. I figure that if he's too absorbed to hear me, I can let him be. For a second I think I'm going to have to, but then he looks slowly back. He smiles around the pencil, then removes it from his mouth. "What's up?"

"You're working on something new?"

He twirls the pencil along his knuckles. "Always. The notes never shut up if I don't write them down."

"Can I hear it?" I ask, even though I didn't intend to.

"It's not done," he says, but he turns back to the keyboard, puts down the pencil, and places his fingers in what I assume are the right spots.

Then he starts to play.

I can taste moonlight, feel the warmth of fur, and smell the pine scented breeze. How is he doing that? The music shifts, an element of discord sliding gradually into the piece. Then the harmonies pull together in a new way and suddenly the song is about hope and something bittersweet.

It ends abruptly.

"I think the next part is something like this."

He plays a moment more, but the spell was broken at the pause.

"That's really good, Seth." I mean it too. I've heard other songs he's written, but something about this one makes those other efforts, which were all superb at the time of listening, seem lacking. "What inspired it?"

He picks the pencil up again and taps it against his papers, looking like I'd just asked him to tell me his deepest secret. Maybe I have.

"Sorry," I say. "It sounds like something personal."

"Yeah." He nods. He places the pencil on the stool beside him and starts to play again. This time the music is less soulful, less full of meaning. If I'd heard it first, I would have thought it excellent, but now it seems a little shallow. Nevertheless, it's catchy enough I find myself humming along.

"I keep thinking to put words to this one," he says, still playing. "But it's about Amber, and I can't really think of the right words for her."

"Your sister does defy description."

He grunts and plays on for another few minutes. Now that he's told me it's his sister's song, I can see her in it. She sways and laughs along with the tune. It makes me wonder what I'd sound like as a song. Part of me wants to ask, but I remind myself why I came here.

"So..." I say. "I've been wondering if I should tell Troy about last night."

"Ah." He switches to something slow and thoughtful. "Well, on one hand, if you're not going to tell him, then what did we go hunting for? On the other hand, it might make more sense to tell Mr. Atherton."

I wince at the thought. "But then I have to admit I left the grounds. Like we were specifically told not to do this month."

"There is that." A few more notes flow by. "I could tell him. Not mention you."

"You'd do that?"

He shrugs.

But, no. I can't let him get himself in trouble and leave me out of it. "It was my idea. I should be the one to tell."

"I could have stopped you."

My eyebrows go up. "Could you really?"

The piano falls silent as Seth grins over his shoulder at me. "Hey, I won most of our fights in cat-form."

Most of them. Not all. That bothers me now that I stop to think about it. My arms fold over my tummy, holding in a sick feeling. "It would be better if you beat me all the time, you know. Dan Rutherford's better than I am, and all it takes is one loss."

He turns further, bringing his legs around the bench. His unspeakably blue eyes latch onto mine, full of sincerity. "You may not believe this, but I would have beat you every time if I wasn't scared to death of hurting you."

Is that true? Had he been so afraid of harming me that he'd let me beat him? It was possible... really possible, in fact. We stare at each other as I try to figure out what to say.

"Anyway..." he says after far too long. His eyes suddenly fall away from mine. "Maybe we should tell Becky. See if she'll tell Atherton without saying who gave her the information."

It's a good idea, so we leave the music room and go to her office. Seth carries the stack of papers with him and reads them as he walks, giving him an excuse not to talk to me. Or maybe he's not avoiding me and just wasn't ready to be pulled out of the world of music yet. I can't let myself think the world revolves around me.

Becky frowns as I start my story, but doesn't interrupt. Her unhappy expression intensifies as I continue, until she ends looking furious.

"You know better than that," she says when I'm done. "We trusted you to stay safe, and you violated that trust."

My insides quiver and nausea curdles my stomach. "I know."

"It wasn't her fault," Seth says. "It was my idea."

"No, it wasn't!" I counter.

The counselor moves her focus between the two of us. "I honestly don't care whose idea it was. Neither of you should have acted on it. There are already search parties out there. Adult search parties. This isn't *Scooby Doo*. We don't need a pack of teenagers to solve the mystery of the all-were."

Seth and I stay silent, waiting for the verdict that likely waits at the end of the tirade. Becky didn't promise not to tell Mr. Atherton where she got her information, but had insisted on hearing what we had to say first. She lets out a long sigh and removes her glasses to rub at her eyes.

"Okay," she says eventually, putting her glasses back on. "I'll cover for you this time. But you have to promise me that you'll stay put from now on. Because if you go out again and get hurt, that'll be my fault for not making sure you were both locked in the building. Do you understand?"

We nod.

"Yes, ma'am," I whisper.

"Ma'am?" She says something under her breath that I suspect I'm not meant to hear. It rhymes with "ducking bell."

"We'll stay on grounds," Seth says, his voice firm.

Becky meets his eyes, and some of the tension leaves her shoulders. "And I don't want you to tell anyone else about this. The last thing we need is for more people to get it into their heads that they should be running around after this girl and whatever spooked her."

"Not even Troy?" I ask.

"Especially not Troy!" For the first time ever, my counselor looks appalled by something I've proposed to do. "Tell him you didn't find anything when you went out like he asked."

I nod before I realize I'm confirming a suspicion. I hadn't told her Troy put me up to the search.

"Now, get going," Becky says. "Before I start yelling at you, and people start asking why."

We get going.

In the hallway, we look at each other.

"Could have been worse," Seth says.

It could have, indeed. Yet tears still sting my eyes. "I've never made her mad before."

Seth puts an arm around me and gives me a half-hug. My heart nearly stops. "You just scared her, that's all."

Stiffly, I nod. "I know. But... Simone hates me now, and I don't think I could handle losing any more of my support network."

"Simone doesn't hate you." Seth's arm falls away, and I suppress a shiver. "She's just throwing one of her tantrums. She'll get over it."

I'm not so sure about that. "Maybe."

"In the meantime, you need breakfast."

"I guess."

"There's no guessing." He puts a hand against my back and nudges me along. "My sister says you're not eating enough."

"Your sister exaggerates."

"True. But I'm still making sure you have breakfast."

So I let him lead me to the dining room, where he eats a massive pile of waffles and watches me force some cereal down. With the moon full, I should be hungrier than I am, but if he hadn't made me come in here, I'd have skipped the meal.

Sam Fox comes in, sees us, and waves. She doesn't look even slightly jealous to see him with someone else, and she doesn't cross over to where we sit. She goes to her usual place, where she's soon joined by her usual crowd, minus Seth. At some point over the last few weeks, he became a normal fixture at her table, but no one looks upset that he's somewhere else. Maybe normal friends don't have fits if you eat with other people; I wouldn't know.

A few minutes later, Bryce enters and takes the seat beside Sam. I can't tell what they say, but they don't do anything to indicate they're a couple. And Seth doesn't so much as blink at them sitting together. So I still don't know what's going on with all of them.

Unfortunately, I know all too well what's going on with me. And that's that I'm being glared at by my best friend. Former best friend? The correction hurts too much for me to acknowledge it. There's a proverb in Russian that says friendship is like glass: you can't mend it once it's broken. I've never believed that, but if I'd let myself, I'd be wondering if our relationship has been shattered beyond repair.

Simone strides straight to my table and stops with a hand on one hip. She hasn't gotten her food yet, so she's free to wave the other hand in the air. "I don't have words for you two. You're just too disgusting."

Seth puts down his fork and meets her glare with a calm look. "And yet, you speak."

"You have a lot of nerve." Simone sneers down at us as the room falls silent, everyone clearly listening to her. "You are still my fiancé, Seth. Even if you are running off into the woods with this slut."

Very slowly, Seth rises to his feet. I don't recognize the glint in his eyes; it's something too menacing for him to have ever directed it at me. "You can say whatever you want about me. But if I ever hear another insult like that aimed at Rina, I'll make sure you never talk to anyone ever again."

This time, I think maybe my heart really does give up on beating. My lungs skip the whole breathing thing as I stare at Seth. There isn't a single part of me that doesn't believe he'd follow through on that threat. From the utter stillness of the room, I think I'm not alone.

Chapter Fifteen

Simone isn't in the clearing when we arrive that night. The others don't mention it, so I don't either, even though I worry about her. I've been worrying a lot today. Simone's obviously more than mad enough to tell Atherton we left last night. Although when I told Seth that, he pointed out that she didn't actually know how far away we went. She seemed to assume Amber was visiting Raja and had left the two of us alone. I don't know where she got the idea from. Even though wild snow leopards aren't pack animals, it's not uncommon for us to go hunting as a group. Why wouldn't she assume we'd all done that?

Seeing my expression, Amber gives me a hug. It's nice and warm, but a stupid voice in my head insists that I'd rather be hugged by her brother. What is wrong with me this moon?

Tonight, Amber and I take turns attacking Seth. He does better against her, and I'm left wondering if it's because she's not as good as I am, or because he cares less about making her bleed. I'm very aware now when he fights me that he holds back, like he thinks I'm fragile.

My lips curl back from my teeth after a particularly lame swat.

He cocks his head like he's confused at the aggression.

I launch at him, seriously trying to get a mouthful of his throat, and in his surprise he clocks me hard enough against the head for the world to spin. That's more like it! I tackle him with renewed vigor and we roll in the snow, not stopping until we're both bleeding.

With a sense of satisfaction, I yield to teeth against my throat.

He lets me go, and I sit down a few feet away to lick the wound on my forearm. He bit me! I might not be happy about that in the morning, when I'll have a throbbing gash and a bruise to show for it, but right now I'm thrilled that I broke him out of his must-protect-the-girl stance.

He huffs and sits beside me, his chest expanding rapidly as he catches his breath.

Amber rolls her eyes and lies down, tucking her tail over her nose and closing her eyes. Clearly, she thinks we're done for the night. She's probably right.

Seth butts his nose against my shoulder, and his eyes drop to the wound I'm cleaning. He touches his nose to just above it, clearly apologizing. Silly male. I'm not apologizing for the wounds I gave him. I lean against him, trying to communicate that there are no hard feelings.

We sit beside each other and lick at our cuts until we're both satisfied they've been taken care of. Then we lie beside Amber. Initially, we're on either side of her like last night, but as I start to drift to sleep I feel a new warmth on my other side and realize Seth's moved to put me in the middle. I wonder why, but I'm too close to sleep to think about it.

Amber is the one who shakes me awake shortly after moonset. Her brother is across the clearing practicing his martial arts poses. His shifts have grown graceful from familiarity, but why is he doing that at two in the morning? Does he usually stay up nights exercising out in the cold?

"He only has a month left," Amber says softly. "I think that's finally sinking in."

I bite my lip. A month isn't much time. Not that it's news to me that we don't have long to train. We're halfway through though, time wise. Are we that far educationally?

"I'm trying to find other ways out of this," she goes on. "But with one side contesting the Challenge... Do you think your parents could help?"

"My parents?" I frown at her as I dig my gloves out of my coat pocket. "Maybe. But why would they?"

"Do they really want the alliance?" she asks.

I'd never really stopped to think about it. "Doesn't everybody? I mean, we were fighting before it."

"Yes." Her folded arms tighten more as she visibly shivers. "But it was a three-way fight. What did Clowder Andreyushkina gain?"

Andreyushkina gained the right to send their first-born daughter to another country, to be raised by another Clowder. I'm a surety against my family's potential aggression. But what did my mother earn other than an excuse to back out of Alaska?

Amber shivers again. "Seems to me that if anyone should have been engaged to my brother, it should have been you."

I laugh, sending a huge puff of condensation out into the air. "Then he'd be fighting my mom. She's even worse than Simone's dad."

"Except he wouldn't be fighting her."

I squint. "I know I'm not as prickly as Simone, but I really don't think it would make a difference. Trapped is trapped."

"Only if you want out," she counters.

"Well, of course he'd still want out."

She waves a hand through the air. "Okay, fine. Would you contest it?"

"Of course not."

"There you go then." She rubs her arms vigorously, then yells her brother's name. "It's freezing out here, you moron!"

He startles, like he's surprised to find that we're here.

We go inside, and I go back to sleep in my nice, warm bed. I can't stop thinking about what Amber said though. Could my family somehow help? Maybe, but I'm not sure what they could do that wouldn't cause serious political backlash.

I make a phone call the next day.

"What's wrong?" my mother asks in Russian. I seldom call rather than email, and never on a weekday.

"I'm fine," I assure her. "But... do you know that Simone's engagement is being Challenged?"

There's a moment of silence during which I start to wonder if the call was disconnected. "Everyone has heard of this."

It takes me a second to realize she's switched to English. There must be someone in the room with her.

"Is there anything we can do to help Seth?"

"He is the boy, yes? The one who does not want your foster-sister."

"Yeah."

She grunts. "There is nothing I can do for him."

"Are you sure?"

"Yes, my love. I am certain there is nothing I can do for him."

I pick up on the emphasis in her words. "So there's something I can do?"

Silence.

"Mother?"

She sighs loudly. "My precious child, I agreed to the arrangement. There is nothing I can do, or tell you to do."

I squeeze my eyes tight. "You said that already. And I get that you won't tell me to do anything. But why won't you tell me what I can do?"

"I will send you a copy of the treaty."

"I don't need the treaty! I need advice!"

"My advice is for you to read the treaty."

Ugh!

We say quick goodbyes, and I hang up frustrated and confused. She really sounded like she was trying to tell me something; and she must not have wanted whoever was in the room to know she was doing it, or she wouldn't have changed into English. But why not tell me outright? Why make me try to guess what she meant?

I take my breakfast tray to Amber and Raja's table so I can tell them about the conversation.

"Dang it." Amber taps her fingers on the side of her glass of orange juice. "When I asked my parents why they refused to intervene, I was told the same thing. Read the treaty."

"Did you?" Raja asks.

"Yeah. It's pretty clear that Seth and Simone are engaged. I didn't see any loopholes."

I sink glumly into my chair. I'd hoped there would be something in the treaty that gave Seth an easy out. "So maybe they're just telling us to live in the real world?"

Amber clicks her tongue as she thinks. "But if they're doing that, why not just lecture outright?"

She has a point. My mother has never backed down from informing me that I have to abide by formal agreements before. That's exactly what she did when I'd call her in tears begging to come home back before I got used to my new family. What's different this time? "And if they do see a way out, if that's why they aren't lecturing us, then why don't they say what it is?"

"Oh, that's simple," Amber says. "There's a clause in the treaty promising not to interfere with it being carried out."

Raja makes a thoughtful sound. "So, maybe they see a way out but can't say what it is. Do you still have your copy of the treaty?"

Amber and I take advantage of not having classes on the days of the full moon and spend the morning pouring over the dry legalese of the document on Amber's laptop. Our parents are referred to throughout as various parties, but it's very clear about the younger daughter of the party of the first part being promised in marriage to the son of the party of the second part. It's obviously not legally binding in the United States, but it is binding within the were-community. As far as I know. "Maybe we should ask someone else to read it. You know, someone who understands this kind of thing?"

Amber stares at me. "You mean, show it to a non-snow leopard?"

Put like that, the idea does sound colossally bad. "Well, if it were a human legal document and you wanted a way out of it, you'd hire a lawyer, right?"

"Yeah..." One of her canines digs into the outside of her lip.

"So, why is this different? Maybe an outside party would have a new perspective."

"But, a non-snow leopard? I've felt weird enough talking about the thing in front of Raja, let alone letting someone read it."

"I get that." And I do. In fact, I feel the same way. "But as long as the reader's still a were, isn't it still inside the community?"

Her responding look is flat. "You know our parents would never see it that way."

"We don't have to tell them we took it to someone."

She laughs. "You're getting devious. I like."

"I'm serious." I lean back in my chair and push against the table.

"But what if they find out?" Amber asks. "It's been a while, but people have been killed for that kind of thing."

"For betraying the were-community, sure."

"For betraying their Clowders." She folds her arms and shakes her head. "It's my brother we're talking about, so you know I don't want to argue. But taking this outside the Clowders could get us ostracized, or worse."

"And fighting could get Seth killed!"

She goes absolutely still. "Not if he has the sense to yield when he's beaten. Dan's going to try to keep him alive. There's no marriage if he's dead."

That's a decent point. "True. But..."

"We just need to read it again. And again. Until we see what our parents are trying to show us."

I give in to my natural tendency to yield. "Yeah, alright."

But is that the right call? I can't stop wondering about it as the moon starts to wane and people settle back into their less-excited selves.

Chapter Sixteen

"I'm going crazy," Troy tells me one morning over breakfast. "If I don't get out of this building, I'm going to snap."

"We all feel that way," I assure him. It's pretty much true. Since the moon, we've all been confined indoors. Even the classes that are usually held outside have been held in the great room. It really sucks, to say the least.

"You seem fine."

"I seem tired," I correct. Between increasing training time with Seth, rereading the treaty every night, searching the Internet for clues about all-weres or skinwalkers, taking care of the half of the freshman class that caught the most recent cold, and seeing a rise in my homework level, I've been lucky to get half as much sleep as I need. And what I do get is riddled with nightmares about Simone. "I'm so exhausted I'm thinking I'll not go on the Anchorage trip Saturday, but stay here and sleep all day."

"Still, you have a choice. I don't."

"Seriously?" It hadn't occurred to me that he wouldn't be allowed to go on the all-school shopping trip. If anyone needs to buy things for the equinox dance, it's him. He still has only three sets of clothes.

"Atherton seems to think I'm a flight risk."

"But if you were going to run off, you'd do it here. Not in Anchorage."

"Word," he mutters. "Although there's not much point here. You said there was no trace of the other skinwalker."

My guts twist. I hate that I lied to him, but I'm saved from having to say anything to make it worse by Penny and Madison, who slide into chairs opposite each other.

"Ugh," says Penny. "If I hear one more teacher say 'Since you don't have anything else to do with the lockdown...' I swear I'm going to go feral. I haven't had this much homework since ever."

"Tell me about it." Madison gives her cereal a stir. "It's the second semester of my senior year. I should not have this much work to do."

"Are you guys going on the trip this weekend?" I ask them.

Penny nods while Madison tells me, "Of course. Isn't everyone?"

Troy snorts. "Some of us weren't invited."

Her eyes wide, Penny stares at him. "That's ridiculous!"

"True though." He scoops up a fork full of eggs and shoves them in his mouth.

"Do you want us to pick something up for you?" Madison asks. I can see her mentally going through the list of stores she'll hit up for men's clothing. "Just give me your sizes."

"Thanks," he mutters around a piece of bacon, not sounding particularly appreciative. "I don't have the money anyway, though."

"Don't worry about it." It's easy for Madison to say things like that, considering the amount of money her family has. Both my birth family and my adoptive one are pretty well off, but hers makes them look dirt poor.

He narrows his eyes at her.

"You can pay me back," she offers. "You'll work over the summer, right?"

"If I'm lucky." I can tell from the cloudiness of his expression that he doubts his luck, and it occurs to me I have no idea what his plans for the summer are. I kinda doubt he has any.

"Then pay me back in the fall." Madison smiles like it's all settled, and I get the suspicion that she'll be buying things for him whether he gives her his sizes or not. No one points out that Madison won't be attending North Sky in the fall.

Thomas and Marie show up, and conversation goes back to the increase in our workload. The teachers all know we're all restricted to the building, but none of them want to acknowledge that their peers are also overloading us. No, they all act like they're the only one to be taking advantage of our circumstances to give us bigger assignments. It wouldn't be so bad if it really were only one or two people doing it, but they're all doing it. If they're not careful, the student body is going to go on strike.

Discontent aside, we struggle on toward the weekend. At last some of my teachers take pity on us and give us only enough homework to take up all of Sunday, leaving Saturday free. Everyone except Troy seems to be going on the trip, making me all the more reluctant to go. I'd love to get out of the building, but I don't want to abandon my friend just to go to a mall. It's not like I particularly enjoy shopping, or feel a need to buy anything new for the upcoming dance.

"You should go," Troy tells me. "I'm just going to be reading more boards. I'll let you know if I find something we haven't already hit fifty times."

He's moved on from static websites to cruising message boards for skinwalkers, but still isn't having much luck. He's found a couple of people claiming to be skinwalkers, but none seem to be credible. I've gotten the feeling that the real all-weres aren't on the Internet any more than the real were-snow leopards are.

It takes a while, but eventually I convince Troy I honestly don't want to go on the school outing to the mall, and we head into the library as the buses head out Saturday morning. To my surprise, Seth sits at a table with a large book open. His hair is loose and it spills around him like a hooded cloak. I resist an urge to go touch it.

He looks up as we enter and gives me a confused smile. "You're not going out?"

"Obviously," Troy answers for me.

Seth glances at him, then back to me. "Okay. Dumb question. What are you up to?"

"Research," I say. "I'm wanting to read up on some Native American shapeshifter myths."

My fellow snow leopard nods like he expected as much. "I'm researching historic Challenges."

My eyebrows go up. That sounds like a better use of time than what I was going to do, although Troy may disagree. "Have you found much?"

"Not really. Most of the histories are oral." He gestures to the book beside him. "But I did find a history from about a century ago that talks about some of the major ones. So far, it's been interesting, but not terribly helpful."

"Sounds like the Native American mythology books," I commiserate. "If the truth about the all-weres is hidden in them, I don't know that I'll recognize it when I read it."

Troy glares at me. "Well, if it's such a hardship, do something else."

"I didn't..." I look between the two boys. Seth won't meet my eyes anymore, but Troy looks straight into them. His jaw is tense and his lips press firmly together. What on Earth is he so upset about? "It's not that I don't want to help you-"

"It's just that I'm not a leopard. Got it." He turns and stomps over to the computer.

I look back to Seth, who shrugs.

If I didn't know any better, I'd think Troy was jealous. But he still looks at Michaela like she's a goddess, so it can't be that. Can it?

I do my best to ignore both boys and go find the next book on my to-be-read list, even though I doubt it will be any more helpful than the last two. I plop onto the couch and begin to read, looking up every now and then to check on my companions.

The thirtieth time or so that I look at him, I find Seth looking back at me. He smiles softly and says, "I'm going to break for lunch."

It's a clear invitation and even though I've only been here for an hour, I find myself hungry, so I nod and put my book down.

"You coming, Troy?" I ask as I stand up.

He waves a hand behind him. "Nah. You go on."

Maybe later I can get him alone and ask what's up with him today. For now, I follow Seth to the student kitchen, where he grabs a jar of jelly from the fridge. "PB&J?"

"Sounds good."

"So..." he says as he pulls down the bread. "I don't think Troy likes me much."

I grab the peanut butter from its cupboard and bring it over to the bread. "You say that as if it's not mutual."

He shrugs and puts two plates down on the counter. "I just have a hard time getting over what he did to Mike and Kim."

"They forgave him though."

"Yes..." He stares at the knife in his hand. "But does it matter if the victims forgive him? Would you feel the same way if he'd raped them?"

"He wouldn't do that."

The stare shifts over to me. "Really? Because as I see it, he violated their bodies without permission. How's it different?"

The answer "it just is" doesn't seem sufficient, so I don't know how to respond.

Seth's eyes break away from me, and he twists the peanut butter open. "I've had this discussion with Mike. She thinks it makes a difference that he supposedly did it out of love."

"But you don't."

He looks back to me for a second before returning his attention to the sandwich preparation. "Again, would that matter if it was rape? What if it was domestic abuse? Would saying he only hit her because he loved her redeem him?"

"I guess not..." I lean against the counter, looking sideways at Seth as he spreads the condiments. "But how is it your place to judge him? The Elders already did."

"True." He puts the top pieces of bread on the sandwiches, then starts to cut them into triangles. "I just would have sent him to North Pole is all. And he doesn't seem to appreciate how lucky he is to be here and have friends like you."

"I think he does. He just doesn't express it every second of the day."

"Well, I guess you'd know better than I do." He tries to smile at me as he hands me my sandwich, but it doesn't quite work.

"Thank you," I say, indicating the food.

Something in Seth's expression seems haunted as he takes the jelly back to the fridge, and it stays there while we take the plates and a packet of chips each to the dining room. I leave my plate to go get us drinks and watch him closely as I walk back. His eyes are on the plate, but he looks more like he's studying something than looking at a sandwich.

"You okay?" I ask as I sit down.

He picks up his sandwich but doesn't look at me as he says, "Yeah. Of course."

There's no way I'd ever buy that. It seems too nosy to pry, but I do it anyway. What can I say? I'm a cat. "Something's wrong. What is it?"

His lips twitch. "You're as bad as my sister."

"I'll take that as a compliment." I take a bite of my PB&J. It has the perfect ratio of peanut butter to jelly. The ones I make are always off in one direction or the other. I wait for him to speak, but he doesn't. So I swallow and ask, "Is it the Challenge? No one would think less of you if you backed out."

"I'd think less of me." He smiles sadly. "But, no, it's not that. Not that it fills me with joy to have it looming, but, you know..."

"So is it Sam?"

His eyebrows draw together. "Sam?"

"I mean, she and Bryce..."

He laughs. "Yeah. No. I'm happy about her and Bryce. Honest."

I just look at him until he starts laughing harder, then I feel compelled to ask, "Are you protesting too much?"

He shakes his head. "No. I promise. My feelings for Sam Fox are entirely platonic."

My eyebrow rises as my mouth presses into a disbelieving frown. Something about it makes Seth laugh even more.

"Trust me. It's been tested."

Tested? "You mean you kissed her as an experiment?"

He stops laughing and shifts, clearly uncomfortable. "Not exactly."

"But you did kiss her?"

Those oh-so-blue eyes of his roam over my face. "Yes."

For some reason, the food in my stomach suddenly feels like a metal weight pulling me into the ocean.

"Do you care?" he asks, so quietly I can almost pretend not to have heard him.

"Of course not. She isn't my type," I answer in a glib attempt to cover up the unease the question gives me. "Red heads are too high maintenance."

His shoulders slump a little at the response and he looks down to his plate. There's only one triangle left, but he doesn't pick it up for a moment. I'd give a lot to know what he's thinking as he gazes at the sandwich, but I'm too scared to ask.

Chapter Seventeen

The days pass in a slow flutter of activities, and the moon wanes smaller. My dreams become more agitated and less restful as the week progresses. I can't remember most of them, but the ones I do are horrible. In one, Troy attacks me, and I can't fight back. In another, it's Seth who's attacked, and I can't see by whom. The most disturbing is the one where Seth and Troy are both killed by Simone, who walks around the school with a butcher's knife and a bloody grin like she's in a horror film.

By the time the equinox arrives, dark bags puff up under my eyes, and I'm starting to feel sleep deprived. Yet, somehow, I still don't have the time to do all of my homework. Or maybe it's the energy I'm lacking. Either way, I miss several assignments and earn a few disappointed looks from my teachers. I'm not used to disappointing teachers.

Exhausted though I am, I don't even think about lessening the number of workouts I do with Seth. In fact, I increase their number and reissue my invite to Troy to join them. Or you might could say I begged Troy to join them, worried as I was that Seth was letting his desire not to hurt me get in the way of training. And, sure enough, my fellow snow leopard proves much more aggressive toward Troy. Aggressive enough that I make a point of not leaving the two of them alone. Therefore, I'm surprised to show up early and see that Seth beat me into the gym Saturday morning.

He smiles widely when I walk in, and I try to smile back.

"You need to go back to bed," he says.

"You're not getting off that easy."

We fall into our routine of stretches followed by poses and then glide into sparring. It's not my best showing, and Seth levels me several times before backing up and giving me a concerned frown. Before he can say anything though, the door opens, and Troy cruises in with an apology for being late.

Seth grunts like he would have rather Troy not showed up at all. That's pretty much been his attitude all week, although he hasn't complained out loud.

I cede my place to Troy and let the boys face off.

With folded legs, I sit against the wall and watch their interaction. Their moves are rapid and strong. Seth might not particularly enjoy spending time with Troy, but he holds back a lot less against the other male than he does with me, and that's indisputably good for him.

My attention wanders for a few moments as I lean back and try not to fall asleep. I don't know why I'm so tired. Part of it is PMS, which always makes me sleepier than usual, but most months it's not this bad. Slowly, my eyes drift shut.

I snap back to the action as two thumps are followed by a hiss of pain.

My eyes widen at Troy, who has shifted his hands into claws. The hiss was from Seth, who crouches several feet away and looks like he's about to lunge at the all-were. Bloody streaks on his arm speak clearly to what I missed.

"Troy!" I yell.

The sound gets him to look my way, which lets Seth tackle him around the stomach without contest. They go down together, Seth pinning Troy down. As I stare in shock, Seth pulls back his arm and his fist crashes into Troy's face.

"Stop it!" I leap up and rush forward to try to get between them as Seth brings his arm back again.

This time, Troy dodges the worst of the punch, taking the blow on his cheek rather than his nose.

"Seth!" From behind, I wrap my arms around him, and he allows me to pull him back.

We stand with my front pressed against his back, my head turned against his shoulder to let me breathe. He drags in deep breaths, his muscles trembling. His body radiates heat and despite everything, a part of me melts into his scent.

"Go," he growls.

Troy laughs. "Is that what you think, Rina? That I should go?"

Why is he laughing?

Not sure it's a great idea, I slowly let go of Seth and take a step to the side. My left hand trails behind me, staying on Seth's back. Troy's nose sits at the wrong angle and a trickle of blood leaks down. Nothing a quick setting and a few hours won't fix, but not something I would personally find funny if it happened to me. "It's probably a good idea. You should go see Nurse Sakura."

"Alright." He rubs the blood from his upper lip and gives me a lopsided smile. "See you tonight, then? Pick you up at seven?"

Seth tenses.

"Yeah. Sure." I'd almost forgotten we were supposed to go to the dance together. I need to figure out where my pink satin dress is.

Troy touches his forehead in mock salute and leaves the room.

As the door closes behind the all-were, Seth lets out a breath and loosens his shoulders.

I withdraw my hand from him, and fight the urge to put it back. "What did I miss?"

"I think you fell asleep." Seth's voice is rough, and I realize that although Troy's departure eased some of his tension, he's still not relaxed.

"Maybe." I move around to face him as I wait to see if he'll elaborate. "Seriously, what happened? Why did he attack you?"

He winces. "I may have started it."

"Why?"

His eyes on the floor, he shakes his head. "He just said some stuff. He has no idea when to shut up."

Some stuff? Must have been some pretty bad *stuff* to result in what I just saw. "Something about Michaela?"

Seth's brow furrows. "No."

"Sam?"

He doesn't say anything, but he makes a negative sounding murmur.

"And if it was Amber, I wouldn't have been able to stop you..." I bite my lip in thought.

"I don't want to talk about it," he says. He walks over to a treadmill and steps onto it. "I'm just going to run for a while."

Okay... "I'll join you."

We run for close to an hour, but he never does tell me what the fight was about. I guess I didn't really expect him to, although I'd love to know. Maybe I'll have more luck asking Troy when I see him later.

We part ways after our run and I traipse upstairs feeling like I'm nearly dead. A shower helps, but then I get into schoolwork and wind up falling asleep at my desk. When I wake up again, it's already dark and someone is knocking on my door.

"Oh my God!" Penny says when I open the door. "You haven't even started getting ready!"

My vision is blurry until I wipe my hand against my eyes and free them of sleep. Penny wears a knee-length copper dress that really goes well with her dark skin. She's in heels and makeup, and has her hair pulled up in a stylish knot. I, on the other hand, am in sweats. "What time is it?"

"Six fifty." She purses her perfectly painted lips at me.

"Crap."

Penny laughs. "That might be the closest I've ever heard to you cursing."

I wave her into the room and rush to my closet while she closes the door behind her. I've already established that the dress I want isn't hanging with the rest of my clothes, but I shuffle through everything anyway.

"You don't even know where your dress is, do you?" Her eyes sparkle as I look back at her. "Girl, you're hopeless."

I look back to the closet. Maybe there's something else that will work. I have a knee-length pleated gray skirt that's pretty nice, and which I pull out. Do I have anything to go with it?

"No," says Penny. "You are not wearing that. You'll look like a librarian."

"It may be that or this." I gesture down my body at my snowflake-covered lounge attire.

She sighs. "What were you planning to wear? Not that."

"No." I put the skirt back. Everything else I own is pants, other than a couple of formal dresses that would be too dressy for tonight... Hey... "It's under the bed!"

"Under the bed?"

I scurry over and pull out a shallow box. It has the dresses I've already worn to things this year in it. "That's where I put stuff I've worn recently. I wore this to-"

"The autumn equinox. I remember." She sounds absolutely exasperated. "You can't wear the same thing tonight."

"Why not?" I rummage through the box until I locate the pink satin. "If anything, it's more appropriate for spring."

"Because you wore it this year!"

"It's not like Troy knows that."

She groans in frustration.

"And I don't have anything else," I point out. "Except other stuff I've also worn this year."

Penny takes a hold of my arm and pulls me toward the door. "Come with me. I have something that'll work."

As we walk to her room, she mutters under her breath about cluelessness and micromanaging. We pass several people in the hall, all closer to ready than I am, and a few smile at me. I can't tell if they're being friendly, or if I'm comical.

Ushered into Penny's room, I shuffle anxiously near the door. "Really, I'm sure the dress I have is fine. It's just an equinox dance, not a big formal."

My words have zero effect on my friend, who flips through her own closet while clucking her tongue. "Maybe... No... What about..."

Finally, she laughs and pulls something out.

I stare at it, shaking my head. "Uh-uh. No way."

"Yes way!" She holds the dress up in front of me, eying the way it looks. "Total win."

"Total fail," I argue. The dress she's picked out is a nice black velvet with little flowers embroidered on it, but it's also very short and very low cut. "I don't have the chest for something like that."

She snorts. "All the more reason to wear it. It was too tight on my boobs. That's why I haven't worn it."

"Penny..."

She points at the clock on her nightstand. "You have negative three minutes to get ready. Put the dress on while I fish out the eyeshadow."

"We can't possibly wear the same makeup! Your skin is like five hundred times darker than mine!"

"That's why I said eyeshadow and not foundation, kitten." She goes into the bathroom without looking to see if I'm changing.

I eye the dress. It eyes me back, just as skeptical as I am.

There's a knock at the door, and Troy's voice comes through after it. "Yo, Penny! Do you know where Rina is?"

Crap and double crap.

"I'll be out in a minute!" I yell back as I start to strip.

It's a bad idea and I know it, but I shimmy the dress down over my head anyway.

"See!" Penny says, reappearing. "You look great."

I frown down at myself. The view is of very little but leg and boob. "I should be wearing a bra."

"No you shouldn't. Trust me." She comes up to me and opens up a case of eyeshadow. "Close your eyes."

I obey reluctantly.

"You have black shoes?" she thinks to ask as she attacks my left eyelid.

"No, just gray."

"Gray should work." She moves on to the other eye. "I have a gray scarf we can tie your hair back with to make it look like you're accenting."

At this point, there's no use in arguing with her, so I let her finish up the eyeshadow and get me the scarf. She puts my hair back for me, tying the scarf around it like a headband. The ends flutter down around my shoulders.

"Very nice," Penny proclaims. "Go get your shoes."

"Yes, ma'am," I mumble on my way to the door.

Troy stands in the hallway, wearing black slacks and an emerald green shirt. He straightens when he sees me, his eyes going wide and locking onto my body. He lets out a slow whistle. "That's some dress."

"It's Penny's," I say, rushing past him as I consider taking the scarf from my head and wrapping it around me. Maybe if I put a cardigan on I wouldn't feel so exposed. "And I need shoes."

He follows me, staying a few paces behind, possibly to check out my ass. Maybe I should wear tights.

"I assure you," he says, "shoes are optional. You look great."

"Thanks."

As I pass the stairs, I pass Seth and agilely move to sidestep him. It doesn't stop me from noticing he stops to watch me pass. As do a couple of other guys. I definitely need to be wearing more.

When I finally make it to my room, Troy picks up his pace and makes it to the doorway before I can close him out. He leans against the door jamb and gives me a sly smile. "You're adorable when you're freaked out."

"I'm not freaked out," I lie. My shoes are on the top of my closet, meaning I have to stretch to get them. This brings the dress even higher up my legs. Leggings sound like a really good idea, but I'm sure Troy will laugh at me if I grab them.

But what's worse, a friend laughing at me or the whole school staring at my body all night?

"Shoes only," Penny says from where she's come to stand beside Troy. How did she know what I was planning?

"I'm freezing," I complain. It's not even an untruth now that I stop panicking long enough to think about it. I take my gray cardigan from its hanger and stubbornly pull it on. Its hem comes down lower than the skirt.

"Wuss," Penny proclaims.

"Leave her alone," Troy says. "She's still hot in the sweater."

"Coming through!" comes Amber's voice. "Make way!"

My fellow snow leopard pushes her way into the room. She's wearing black too, but her dress goes all the way to her knees and has full belled sleeves that fall past the tips of her fingers. Her eyes go over me and she nods. "Adorable yet sexy. I approve."

Her eyes drop to my legs. "Are your legs going to get cold?"

I nearly rush over and hug her for giving me an excuse to get leggings. I don't though, and I don't get the leggings either. "No, I'll be fine."

I have no idea why I said that because as soon as I do, I want to take the words back. But everyone looks happy with the answer, so I don't.

Amber draws closer, then puts her arms around me. She whispers as she hugs me. "My brother thought I should check on you. Are you well?"

"Yeah," I whisper back. "Now that I have my cardigan."

Her eyebrows go up as she pulls back, probably imagining what I looked like without the sweater. She nods. "I needs must seek my girlfriend. Shall I see you later? I want to dance with the girl in the short skirt."

I smile, feeling my cheeks heat up as she winks at me. "Alright."

She narrows her eyes at Troy as she turns to leave. "You had best behave."

"Me?" He points to himself like he has no idea why she'd think he'd do otherwise. "I didn't put her in that dress."

"And you're not going to take it off either," Amber says on her way out the door.

"Like I'd ever be so lucky," he counters, sounding a little sullen.

Under normal circumstances, we hold dances in one of the outbuildings, so there's at least a little bit of a "going somewhere" feel to things. With the current lockdown, though, we're having it in the dining room. I don't know where they managed to stack all the tables and chairs.

Shimmering streamers streak across the ceiling, suggesting the Aurora Borealis while holding none of its magic. The usual overhead lights are off, replaced by Christmas lights and fake candles. In the dimness, you could almost mistake the place for a different room. Almost. The thin gray carpet is a bit of a giveaway, even with a wood dance floor covering part of it.

Troy has his hand on my back as we enter the room, his palm spreading warmth through the back of my sweater. If the hand wasn't there, I'm not sure I'd continue walking after people start to notice me. Or, more accurately, after they start to notice my legs. It feels like the whole room is staring at them, even though analytically I notice that most people don't even glance my way.

We cross the room to the refreshments by silent agreement, and Troy hands me a cup of punch. I'd prefer cola, or even coffee, as caffeine tends to have a calming effect on me, but I accept the sugary concoction anyway and try not to wince at the sweetness as I sip it.

I've always been what's known as a wallflower, so it seems natural to me to drift to the side of the room. Troy follows me with a slight frown, and drapes an arm around my shoulders when we come to a stop. "I'm not going to let you decorate the wall all night, you know."

"I'm not very good at dancing," I murmur. "Not this kind anyway. Just ballet."

"Ballet?" He draws in a long breath. "I would watch you dance a ballet. In fact, I bet no one would object if we cleared the floor for it."

"And it would go so well with Lady Gaga," I say, referencing the current music.

He makes a face like he's giving this serious consideration. "Actually, I think it could work. And she'd certainly approve."

"Approve of what?" Penny asks as she appears at Troy's side. Seth trails behind her, staring at his shoes. This is a pity as I'm pretty sure the blue shirt he's wearing would really set off his eyes if he looked up.

Troy squeezes my shoulders before dropping his arm and shifting to put a little more distance between us. "Ballet dancing to Gaga. I think it could be a thing."

"Oh, yeah," Penny agrees. "That would be awesome."

"She doesn't do ballet anymore," Seth says. He looks levelly at Troy. "Not since she broke her ankle a few years ago."

"Ah. Too bad." Troy downs the remainder of his drink and eyes my still-full cup. "Guess you'll have no choice but to dance like everyone else then."

"She doesn't have to dance," Seth says.

Penny smacks his arm. "She does, too! We all do!"

It's pretty clear that this is a hint, but Seth either doesn't pick up on it or pretends not to. It's possible he's distracted because at the same moment Penny is making her hint, Simone walks through the door looking more beautiful than I've ever seen her.

She's wearing a long strapless dress that clings in all the right ways to all the right places, making me feel suddenly frumpy in my cardigan. She catches me staring at her and gives me what historical romances describe as "the cut" by looking instantly away without acknowledging me. It hurts, but less than it would have a few weeks ago.

I close my eyes for a moment, and when I open then again, Seth is looking at me. I was absolutely right about that shirt and his eyes.

"Come on," Troy says. He takes the cup from my hand, downs the contents, and tosses it into the nearby recycling container. "We're dancing."

"Us too!" Penny chimes, grabbing Seth's arm and pulling him toward the floor right as the song changes to something slower.

Apparently a lot of people were waiting for a slow song, because the wooden boards are suddenly crowded.

Troy puts his arms loosely around me and starts to sway, smoothly at first but then with an odd tension to his posture. I squint up at him, then look at where he's looking.

Ah. Of course. It's Michaela. More to the point, it's Michaela and Warren, pressed close together and looking like they're alone on their own little planet. My heart breaks a little for my friend. He so totally doesn't have a chance.

I should say, or do, something to distract Troy, but nothing pops to mind. Coming here was stupid. "Maybe we should go watch a movie or something."

He looks down at me with a frown. Then he pulls me right up against his chest and places his cheek against the top of my head. "I'm sorry. I'm really messed up. Thank you for putting up with me."

I have no idea what to say, and settle for making a small sound just to show I heard him. I'm suddenly feeling really, really warm. I want to pull away from him, escape his heat. But he's holding on tight, like he needs me to be there. His musky scent whirls around me, making it difficult to draw full breaths.

As sweat starts to form a pool at the base of my back, the song ends and another fast one starts up. Never before have I been so happy to hear a quick beat. I jump back away from Troy, trying to hide the action beneath a dance step. My foot lands funny and my ankle rolls me to the side. Next thing I know, I'm falling.

I don't fall far though. Before I can do more than go instinctively limp, Seth is there behind me. His arms grab under my elbows to keep me upright. He pulls me up until I'm standing like a normal person and walks around me until we face each other.

"Are you okay?" he asks.

"Yeah." I wiggle my foot. "Ankle's a little sore, but it's not twisted or anything."

His voice drops low. "That's not what I meant."

I look at him, wondering what he sees when he looks at me. His eyes lock onto mine and I start to understand the phrase "lost in his gaze." I'm dimly aware that people are dancing around us, but they hardly register as real.

He leans closer, not even blinking as he whispers, "You smelled terrified."

I jerk back, but don't break eye contact. "What?"

"Before you fell."

Reflexively, I sniff my shoulder. I do smell afraid, but I nevertheless shake my head. "I'm fine."

"Are you sure?"

"Hey," Troy interjects. "She said she's fine. You've already rescued her. Bravo."

Seth's eyes don't so much as flicker toward the other male.

"I'm fine," I repeat, adding an attempted smile. "I just need to sit down for a minute."

They both follow me as I make my way over to a group of chairs under the front windows. I sit in the middle, but neither of them sit with me. Instead, they stand, one on each side of me, and glare at each other. When Penny slides in between them, I nearly break into cheers.

"What happened?" the wolf asks. She can't possibly be oblivious to the tension between the guys, but she does a good job of acting like she doesn't notice it.

I hold my leg out. "Landed wrong and hurt myself. I'll be fine in a few minutes though. It's just sore."

"Oh, good." She puts a hand on Troy's arm. "So you don't mind if I steal your date for a song?"

"Not as long as you return him in good condition."

He doesn't come across as very enthusiastic, but he lets her lead him back to the dance floor.

"You don't have to babysit me," I tell Seth, but he sits down beside me anyway.

He leans forward with his elbows resting on his thighs and stares at the carpet. His mouth opens a few times, like he's going to say something, but he keeps closing it again. Behind him, his hair flows loose like a cloak. I have an unacceptable urge to touch it.

"Are you okay?" I ask him.

He smiles sadly. "Yeah. As long as you are. I just... I..." He leans further forward and his hair falls to hide the side of his face.

I lean forward, trying to see around all the hair. "You..?"

His head shakes ever so slightly.

The temptation to touch his hair overrides my good sense and I reach out to move the closest sheet of it back behind his ear. My fingers stay there, and he goes perfectly still, not even breathing. His scent shifts, the last of his anger fading into something I'm not familiar with. Something dark yet attractive. "Seth?"

His eyes shut as he swallows and draws in some air. Then, ever so slowly, he leans against my hand. My palm flattens against his cheek and my heart is suddenly leaping into my throat.

He draws another breath, then his lips brush against my skin as he speaks. "You don't smell scared anymore."

"I don't?"

He smiles softly. "No."

I can only imagine how I smell now. I can't pick up a hint of my own scent with my nose so preoccupied with his.

"Fight!" someone announces.

Our heads snap up.

"Stop it!" insists a different someone, a much more female someone.

Seth curses under his breath and gets to his feet. He holds a hand out to help me up behind him. My ankle twinges slightly, but I ignore it, because there's no doubt in my mind that we'll find Troy at the center of the disturbance.

Chapter Eighteen

We weave through all the people who were dancing but are now watching the three people standing directly before the refreshment table. Just as expected, one of them is Troy. The other two are Warren and Michaela. The latter has her arms around her boyfriend and seems to be whispering something to him as he glowers menacingly at Troy.

For his part, Troy just stands there. If it wasn't for the fact that his hands have shifted into claws, I'd even say he was standing there looking innocent.

Nurse Sakura wisps through the crowd to arrive before us and inserts herself between Troy and Warren. She's noticeably shorter than either of them, but wears an expression that allows for no argument as she commands them to separate. Everyone knows you do not want to be on the wrong side of a coyote.

As I drift to a stop, my fellow students shuffle in growing disappointment at it looking less and less like there's going to be a fight. To the side, I notice Penny standing with a cowed expression. I'd be annoyed with her, except I recognize that Warren is much higher in their pack than she is. That sort of thing is important to wolves, and it consequently would take a massive amount of bravery for her to get involved.

I meet Nurse Sakura's eyes for a second, and she gestures toward Troy. "He needs a break," she says before turning to deal with Warren.

My hand wraps around Troy's arm, and I pull him away from the scene.

We leave the dining room entirely before Troy wrenches his arm free and stomps over to the stairs. Somewhere during the trip, his hands shifted back into hands. "I didn't do anything."

"Sure," says Seth.

I glare at my fellow snow leopard. "Can the sarcasm."

He holds his hands up in surrender and goes to lean against a wall.

"I swear," Troy says, ignoring Seth and focusing on me. "I didn't do anything. She said hello to me. I said hi back. Then -boom! That asshole was all in my face."

There has to be more to it than that. Even wolves aren't that territorial.

"How did you say hi?" I ask.

Troy squints in disbelief. "What do you mean, how did I say hi? I said, 'Hi.' Like I was passing her in a hallway or something."

Over by the wall, Seth makes a rude snort. "And did you say it to her, or to her breasts?"

I look over, and Seth raises his eyebrows. "Did you notice what Mike was wearing? It's a lot like what you've got on, minus the sweater."

Right. So Troy's ex walked up to him wearing something tight and low cut, then his eyes did what I suspect the eyes of any straight male would do. "That would set Warren off."

"Seriously?" Troy plops down on the stairs. "I didn't do anything. I may have noticed the dress. But I didn't do anything."

"Wolves are a bit on the possessive side," I tell him.

He shakes his head. "Everyone here is on the possessive side."

I shrug. He may have a point. I don't know what it's like with humans, so I can't really say.

"Troy?" We all turn as Michaela walks in, Warren in tow. She runs her tongue over her lip, glances at Seth, then focuses on Troy. "You should come back. We're leaving."

He stares at her sullenly. He is not, I notice, staring at her breasts, even though their display is quite attractive. "No need."

Michaela's eyes flit from face to face, finally resting on mine. "Make sure he goes back. Please?"

I nod, but as she and Warren go down the hall toward the student kitchen, Troy rises and stomps up the stairs. He doesn't look back, and I very much get the impression that he doesn't want to be followed.

My teeth dig into my lip as I consider letting him go. But I can't do it. I rush up behind him and slip into his room before he can close the door.

If I didn't know how North Sky's rooms were decorated, I might think I've stepped into a hotel room. The place is neat as a pin, free of both dust and personalization.

Troy crosses to the window and stands there, gazing at his reflection with an expression I can't read. I take off my shoes so that I can prop the door open with one of them, then limp over to stand near him.

"Why are you here?" he asks. The words aren't welcoming, but the soft and hurt way he says them makes me glad I followed him.

"Because you look like you need a friend."

He snorts and his breath condenses on the glass in front of his face. "And why do you care?"

It's a question designed, I strongly suspect, to make me go away. And I won't lie; I'm tempted to leave. But I'm not going to. "Because I'm a friend."

He turns to look down at me, his eyes probing. "Seriously," he says quietly. "Why are you so damned nice to me? Can't you tell what I am?"

Slowly, I nod. "You're someone who's in pain."

His face cracks, and for a second I think he's going to cry. "I'm someone who causes pain."

"Maybe," I admit. "But we all do that. Does it make us all worthless?"

"You?" He reaches out and strokes my hair, the gentle warmth from his hand nearly making me shiver. "You're not capable of hurting anyone."

"Simone," I state simply, my voice catching on the name.

He pauses in consideration. "You weren't trying to hurt Simone. You were trying to help Seth. And from what I understand, his life could be in danger, which would make helping him more important than protecting her feelings."

"Still, I hurt her. I knew I was going to, and I did it anyway." I look down at the window ledge.

He brushes my hair again, and this time it produces the smallest of trembles. I can't tell if I like the sensation or not, so I shift away. In response, his hand falls to his side and his eyes drop to the floor. He takes a breath and says, "You should go back. Don't let me ruin the party for you."

"I'll go back if you go with me."

His head shakes. "No one wants me there."

"Don't be ridiculous," I say. "Why would Madison and Penny have bought you those clothes if they didn't want you there? And Madison never got a dance."

"I'm not really in the mood for dancing anymore." His hand rises like he's going to touch me again, but he stops himself from actually reaching over. The aborted action makes my heart clench, and I inch closer to him.

His eyes bore into mine.

I swallow and ask, before I can lose my nerve, "Not even with me?"

"Don't tease me," he says softly.

The words lance into me, making me step back. It would be so easy to kiss him now, but I have just enough sense not to. "I wasn't... I didn't mean..."

He lets out a tired breath and turns back to the window. "Just go. Please?"

And despite what I promised Michaela, I do.

Chapter Nineteen

I hesitate in the hallway with my shoes dangling from my hand. I don't know if I should go back down, or turn around and drag Troy from his room. Or maybe stay here with him… but when he accused me of teasing him, I came very close to doing something I don't think I want to do.

No, the best thing to do is not go back. I'll take a series of steps down this hallway, then turn at the stairs. But do I go up to my floor or down to the dance? Uncertain of my destination, I nevertheless start down the corridor, trying to put Troy and any thoughts I may be having about him behind me. I was just responding to his pain is all. I didn't really want to kiss him. I'm almost certain of that.

My ankle stings with each step I take, so I should probably go to my room. It's not like I'll be following through on my promise to dance with Amber anyway.

A whistle shoots through the air. "Earth to Rina!"

I stop, dazed to notice Penny leaning in the doorway I was about to walk blindly past.

"What happened, kitten?" the wolf asks. "What we saw looked pretty intense."

What she saw? It takes me a moment to realize she must have looked into Troy's room from the hall. "Oh. Nothing. He's just upset."

Her expression doesn't show much confidence in the accuracy of my answer, but she doesn't say anything about it as she continues to watch me.

I look past her into the room she's guarding. The walls are covered in sheet music, and I find myself drifting closer in an attempt to read some of it. Seth's scent wafts from inside the room, making sure I know I'm on the edge of his territory. As if anyone else at North Sky would paper their walls with notes.

"It reminds me of your room," Penny says in a tone that is decidedly suggestive of something.

I'm not entirely sure what she's trying to imply, but before I can even look at her funny, she shifts, and I see Seth sitting across the room with his back to the wall. One knee is up before him while the other leg stretches out straight. I narrow my eyes at him. "You okay?"

"Yeah. Of course." His answer is just the slightest bit too fast. He follows it up with a wave of his hand as I wonder what they were talking about before I blundered onto the scene. "We were just waiting to see if you were going back down."

He doesn't get up, and I can't tell what he wants the answer to be.

"I don't know. Troy isn't. I was thinking I might just go rest my ankle."

Seth frowns at my feet. "It's the one you broke before, right?"

"Yeah." I'm impressed that he remembers which ankle I broke. It's not like it spent more than a few days healing. I wiggle it around. "It's not bad though, as long as I don't put too much weight on it."

"That would seem to preclude dancing," he observes.

I shrug. "Yeah, but I'll go back with you guys if you want me to."

Penny swats at me. "Of course we want you to."

"Not if it's going to make the ankle worse." Despite the words, Seth stands as though going somewhere. "We'll do something else. Watch some of your ancient movies or something."

"Movies?" Penny wrinkles her nose at the notion. "We can watch movies any time. Her ankle's not that bad, is it?"

They both look at me, waiting for the final call.

"I don't want to ruin your night," I tell them. "You don't have to stay with me."

Penny slumps. "So you're not coming?"

I shake my head. "Sorry. I should do that rest and elevation thing."

"Okay." They trade a glance, and Penny's lips slide into a subtle smile. "We'll let our white knight here fetch you some ice while I take you upstairs."

Seth's eyes narrow at the title she just gave him, but he accepts the implied order with grace. "Alright. Meet you upstairs."

He ushers us from his room and walks us to the stairs, then he darts down as we start slowly up. The ankle hurts more now, but maybe that's just because I'm thinking about it. I try to think of something else, but the only thing that comes to mind is the fact that I nearly kissed Troy, and I don't want to think about that either.

"There's that expression again," Penny says. "What's it mean?"

"Um... nothing?"

"Right." She gives me a disparaging look as we turn toward my room. "Did he kiss you?"

"What?" I stop to better stare at her. "Why would you ask that?"

"Because he totally looked like he was going to kiss you."

"Well, he didn't."

"Okay." She starts up the hall again, and I limp after her. "Are we upset about that? Because you sound upset about that."

I make a deliberate effort to soften my voice. "No, I'm not. But did it really look like he was going to?"

"Afraid so." She bites her lip for a second. "Are you a lesbian?"

My feet stop moving again.

"Sorry," she says. "I shouldn't have just blurted it out like that."

"You think I'm a lesbian because I didn't want Troy to kiss me?"

"No!" she says quickly. "It's just-" She cuts herself off and stares at me with wide eyes.

"It's just?" I repeat.

She shakes her head. "I just heard a rumor."

"Uh-huh. And who told you this rumor?"

"It doesn't matter."

This is, in my opinion, untrue. I'm guessing Seth said something. If so, that's different than if random people who don't really know me are actually spreading rumors about it. Or I think that would be different anyway… I'm not completely sure how.

"I'll answer the question," I offer. "If you tell me who told you that."

Her breath is long and drawn out. "He didn't mean to tell me. He wasn't gossiping."

"Seth?"

She takes a second before answering, "Yeah."

We walk the rest of the way to my room and slide inside. I shut the door behind us. "I do like girls. And boys. I'm bi."

"Cool! Me, too!" She collapses onto my couch with a grin. "So why didn't you want Troy to kiss you?"

I roll my eyes and limp over to sit beside her. "Do you want every boy you know kissing you?"

"Most of them, sure." She laughs. "Okay, maybe not. But Troy's hot."

"And hung up on his ex," I remind her. "You go be rebound girl if you want."

"So, that's it?" With her head cocked to the side, she watches me closely. "You just don't want to be a rebound?"

No, there's more to it than that. But I'm not sure I want to talk about it. "I just don't think it's a good idea."

A knock on the door saves me from another question, and I call out to Seth that he can come in.

Only after the ice is on my ankle and my friends are gone do I realize I didn't want to be left alone.

A group of freshmen snicker as I walk into the dining hall Monday morning. The paranoid side of me is certain they're laughing at me, but I keep walking rather than give into my instinct to run away.

Madison wears an odd expression when I make it to the wolves' table and the part of me that always expects to be rejected wonders if my open invitation to sit here has been revoked. But she doesn't say anything as I sit down.

The table next to ours hushes to a whisper.

My cereal tastes too bland, and the room seems too loud. Except for the area around me, which remains too quiet.

Troy and Penny arrive, casting curious looks at the other tables.

"What is wrong with everyone?" Troy asks as Penny sits down.

"You haven't heard?" Madison asks. Then she shakes her head in annoyance. "Of course you haven't heard. It's not like anyone would tell you about it."

He gives her a long look as he takes his seat. "About what?"

Madison's eyes move around like she's checking to see if anyone is listening. She leans forward. Then she says in a tiny voice, "What happened after you left the dance?"

Troy's face scrunches. "Nothing. Why?"

"That's not the word."

I lay my spoon down slowly, feeling that I probably don't want to take another bite before she elaborates.

"As I heard it..." She pauses like she's considering not telling us, but eventually goes on. "They're saying you two-" She stops again to indicated me and Troy. "Slipped off together. And went to his room."

"Yeah..." I don't understand why she's blushing.

"Oh," says Penny, apparently catching onto to something I don't see yet.

Madison takes a deep breath. "With the door closed. For hours."

"Huh?" is my immediate response, but then it hits me. "They think we had sex?"

My exclamation makes Troy laugh. Sure, to him it's funny. He's a guy. To me, it's... well, it's not insulting, exactly. Were-culture doesn't generally support slut-shaming, and I'm certain I wouldn't be the only sexually active girl in school, even if I might be one of the youngest. But who likes being accused of things they didn't do?

"Hey!" Penny smacks Troy's arm. "It's not funny."

"Sure it is." Troy says. But he stops laughing and gives me a mildly apologetic look. "Who cares what they think about something that didn't even happen? They're idiots if they're judging you."

"They're idiots anyway," Madison says. She smiles gently. "It's just a rumor. People will get bored of it soon."

Troy dings his spoon thoughtfully against the side of his cereal bowl. "Fifty dollars says Simone's behind it."

"You don't have fifty dollars," Penny points out.

He shrugs. "Fine. No bet. But we should start something horrible about her."

Madison shakes her head firmly. "No. We're better than that."

"And it wasn't her," I say, willing myself to believe it. "It's not her style."

The others trade glances that all but scream their disagreement.

"There's more," Madison says. She pulls her phone out of her pocket and turns it on. After a few presses on the screen, she passes it to me.

The phone shows a picture of me, closing a door with a pair of shoes in my hand. That wouldn't be terribly interesting, but there's text on the photo indicating that it's Troy's door, that it was taken at four in the morning, and alerting all viewers to the fact that my hair is slightly mussed. The real kick to the gut is the little poem under it though.

One, two, three, four.
Close the door,
You little whore.

It's not even a good poem. And things don't get more Simone's style than that.

My eyes squeeze shut as I hand the phone back, but I can smell that it's Penny who puts her arm around me. "It's okay," she whispers.

"What, was she stalking you?" Troy asks. "Standing in the hallway the whole five minutes you were in my room?"

"No," says Penny. "Seth and I would have seen her. It was either a surveillance camera or she just got lucky."

I shake my head in disbelief. As bad as things have been between me and Simone, I guess a part of me still figured we'd work things out eventually. That part is dying.

A new ripple of interest rolls across the crowd, and I open my eyes to see Simone entering. People look between my table and her like they expect a confrontation. Guess we're not the only ones thinking Simone is behind the gossip.

Troy tenses, draws in a breath, and puts down his spoon. I put my hand over his, giving him a slight shake of my head. "She wants us to draw more attention to ourselves. Let it go."

His eyes narrow on me. "You're the one who's upset by all these idiots."

"Right. But confronting her is just going to make it worse."

"So what?" He pulls his hand away from mine. "You're just going to let her get away with doing whatever she wants to you?"

"No..." well, maybe. "Now is not the time to react." If there ever will be a time. Maybe ignoring it really is the best approach. That's how all the old advice about bullies went, wasn't it? Ignore them, and they'll go away. Except I've seen people ignore Simone; she doesn't go away.

"Whatever." He picks his spoon up again and uses it to shove cereal in his mouth.

"It's a good call," Madison says as the tables around us slowly stop paying attention.

Penny tightens her arm briefly before letting go of me and going back to her seat. "A good call for now. I still think that bitch needs some payback."

Troy nods at the declaration, but Madison frowns. "And what do you plan on doing? Spreading a rumor about her?"

"You could just beat her senseless," Troy offers. "I mean, I can't, because she's a girl. But you could do it."

"Or tell Atherton," Penny says pointedly. "She's still on probation from harassing Michaela."

Go to the principal? That could work if we had any proof she was doing it, but I can't imagine she was stupid enough to use a known email account. Maybe she used her own computer though. Can something like that be traced? "We'd need evidence."

Penny grins. "I know just the people."

We finish breakfast quickly and leave en masse. As hoped, Simone doesn't try to stop us. Probably because we outnumber her and Lyly.

"Where are we going?" Troy asks as we walk past the stairs up to our rooms and head into a hallway filled with staff offices.

"The dungeon."

I hesitate at Penny's words. "The Ashes aren't really fans of mine."

Ashe and Ashley are the school's top cybergeeks. Ashe is a male polar bear and Ashley a female fox. They spend most of their time in basement, where the servers are, but when they are seen above ground, they're generally together. Not romantically, as far as I've ever been able to tell, but that doesn't stop people from acting like they're a couple.

"They aren't fans of Simone, you mean," Penny says. "That's not the same thing."

I don't know about that, though. And when we get downstairs Ashley's expression makes me think she doesn't see much difference either. Her hair is a ruddy red, her skin is east-Asian brown, and her eyes are blazing with distrust. "What do you want?"

"Is that any way to treat visitors?" Ashe chides her, getting up from a computer surrounded by Mountain Dew cans. "They come all the way down here to grace us with their presence, and you act like one of them is a recently pariahed, former elitist, snobby pants who deserves everything she's gotten."

"Snobby pants?" Penny repeats with incredulity. "Sorry, I totally missed the regression to elementary school."

"You want more grown up words?" Ashe asks. "I have a few."

He doesn't say them though, a fact that I suspect may be related to the way Troy has stepped up to him with clenched fists. Ashe is unusually lanky for a bear and Troy looks like he could easily snap him in two.

I put my hand on Troy's elbow. "No, he's right. I don't deserve their help. I'm sorry we bothered you."

"Whoa!" Penny sticks her arm out to block my exit. "First off, Rina here was more abused as Simone's friend than you've ever been as her enemies. And secondly, I am presenting you not with an opportunity to help Katerina, but with an opportunity to hurt Simone."

Ashe doesn't look convinced, but he keeps his silence as Ashley says, "Okay. You have my interest."

"Have you seen the meme of the day?" Penny gestures to Madison, who holds up her phone with the screen facing the Ashes.

"Yeah, we've seen it," Ashe says, his voice gruff. "You think it's from Simone?"

Madison smiles sadly. "Who else is that bad at poetry?"

Ashe chuckles as Ashley nods.

"So what do you want us to do?" the vixen asks. "Prove the email came from her? That will be hard. I mean, the IP address will only go as far as the school. It could be from anyone here."

"Unless she's set up a static IP," Ashe says. I have no idea what this means.

"Yeah, but she hasn't. She probably doesn't even know what an IP is." Ashley waves her hand, but stops the action mid-motion. "And I bet she doesn't know how to mask ID on file creation."

Her partner snaps his fingers and rushes back to the desk he abandoned on our arrival. He clicks the mouse a few times, then groans. "Whoever created this image used one of the library computers. ID's as Guest at North Sky. Not helpful."

Troy frowns. "But she didn't take the picture with school property."

"Probably not," Ashe agrees. "But we don't have the original file. She didn't alter the picture to get the words on, she created a whole new file in a meme creator. So without hacking into the email address that sent this, I think we're at a dead end."

"And you can't do that," Madison says.

Ashe's eyebrows go up. "Did I say that?"

"You did not," Ashley responds. She looks at us. "I've never heard of this server, so I have no idea if we could get in or not."

I shiver, conflicted as to whether I should just let the conversation die here. Finally, I opt to speak. "She only has one password."

"What?" Ash bursts out laughing. "Are you serious? And do you know it?"

"Unless she changed it. And she probably didn't because she'd have to change it everywhere."

"Okay," says Troy. "So we can probably get in. Will that prove anything?"

Ashley shrugs. "Maybe. Sometimes, when you create an email address, you have to provide another address to be verified through."

"Huh?" Madison frowns. "So to get an email address, you have to have an email address?"

"Not always." Ashe does some typing and then snaps his fingers at the screen. "But here you do. So if we get in, we'll be able to see the other address. Not really admissible evidence though, since there's always the possibility we created the addresses to frame her."

"Then why would she have verified?" Ashley asks. "It sounds like proof to me."

"Okay, how's this?" Ashe looks over his shoulder at his friend. "I'm not walking into Atherton's office and admitting I slipped into another student's email. Are you?"

"I'll do it," Troy offers.

Madison clicks her tongue. "No, that would still leave the possibility that we did it. If we admit we got into this account by knowing her password, that would mean we could get into any of them."

A glum mood descends over us all.

"Alright," Penny says after a long silence. "So we plan something that doesn't involve telling Atherton?"

My teeth dig into the inside of my lip and a queasiness wells up inside me. The taste of blood hits my tongue, and I realize I've bitten through skin. Like a cartoon character who only falls when he looks down to see nothing there, the pain waits for the realization to hit. I anchor around it and breathe through my nose.

"Oh!" Penny claps. "We go online as her and post really embarrassing things! Or order really expensive stuff and get her in trouble with her parents! Or buy things that are both expensive and embarrassing! Like sex toys!"

"Not bad," Madison says slowly. "But what if we just change her passwords? She won't be able to get into anything. That would drive me nuts."

"I like that," Ashley says. "And she won't be able to reset them because they'll be sending emails to an inbox she can't get to. Then we can make normal sounding posts as her so that when she calls customer service, they'll show normal activity and think the caller is scamming."

Ashe chuckles. "It would be better if she wouldn't get her school account back fast. I mean, Claire will know it's her when she walks into the office and complains her password won't work."

"So it's not perfect," Ashley admits. "It would still be super annoying. And we could combine it with the other ideas. Maybe some of the stuff will ship before she gets the confirmation emails."

A picture of Simone's dad reacting to getting a charge for a thousand dollars worth of vibrators springs to mind. It makes me snicker, but doesn't dent the horrid feeling in my stomach. "I don't know, guys..."

Frowns turn toward me from all directions.

"Why not?" Penny asks.

"I just..." I flounder for words. "It doesn't feel right. I'm sorry."

I run from the room before anyone can stop me, going straight to Becky's office.

Though the door was open, the room is empty. I spin the middle of it, wondering what I should do now. My heart races and tears stream down my cheeks.

Just as I'm about to shut the door to keep people who aren't Becky out, Seth appears in the way. His eyes are frantic as he asks, "What's wrong?" He winces almost immediately. "Sorry. Stupid question. You were just running like someone was chasing you."

I stare at him for a second. It was only a stupid question if he's seen the meme. Which I guess means he has. For some reason I can't fathom, my tears dry up. I think maybe I just don't want to cry in front of Seth. There's no way I can hide the fact that I've been crying, though. Nevertheless, as I turn and walk deeper into the room, I wipe the tears away and try to pretend they were never there.

"It's okay," Seth says as he comes in, closing the door behind him. "No one believes that stupid thing."

I bend my head and let my hair cover the sides of my face.

Seth's hand descends on my shoulder, a warming comfort that I don't deserve. "Even if it were true, she shouldn't have called you that."

No, she shouldn't. But how can I claim the high ground when I was a second away from seeking revenge? "But... It's not just what happened, Seth. It's how I reacted to it."

I turn so that I can see him, and he narrows his gorgeous eyes at me in concentration.

"How did you react?"

It was the obvious question to ask, and I wonder why I left the opening for it. I sit down on a pile of cushions on the couch and hug one of them to me. "I was angry. I wanted to do something to her."

"Seems reasonable to me." He sits on the ground in front of me with his legs folded. "In fact, if you're still plotting revenge, I'd be more than happy to help. But you aren't, are you?"

I shake my head. "No. It's... I don't know."

His lips curve slightly and his look softens. "It's because you're a better person than she is. Or, I'll admit, I am."

"I don't think it's that."

He shrugs. "Then why is it?"

I don't have an answer for him, so I shake my head again. I'm going to make myself dizzy if I don't stop.

There's a knock on the door and less than a second later, it opens to reveal Becky. The bear frowns a little, but doesn't mention that stupid rule that says we should have left the door open. "Hey," she says softly. "How you holding up, kitten?"

I swallow, still managing to refrain from a resumption in crying. "I'm fine."

Her eyes go to Seth, who backs me up. "She's fine."

"Good." Becky sinks into her arm chair. "Do you want to be there when Mr. Atherton talks to Simone?"

"What?" I squint at my counselor.

"So I was right?" Seth asks. He doesn't sound particularly happy about it. "It was Simone?"

"Maybe. Atherton thinks it's likely enough to question her." She pauses for a breath. "He's called in the sorceror. The same one who got her to confess about the barn painting."

She'd never told me what they did to make her crack. If they'd brought in an actual sorcerer to do a truth spell, that would have done it. "But that's too expensive to be worth it."

"No, it's not," Becky disagrees. "Bullying is a very serious issue. The school is not going to let people get away with it. Not this blatantly."

"The blatancy is key," Seth says sardonically. "She's been getting away with things that don't leave a trail for two years."

"Yes, well…" Becky doesn't seem to have an excuse to offer. "It ends here."

"We can but hope," Seth says before he turns back to me. "So, are you going? I think we should."

"Both of us?"

He draws in a slow breath. "I think I should be there. It's my fault she did it."

"I'm not following you…" What does Seth have to do with it? Other than knowing both of us, what's his connection?

"We, um…" His eyes move toward Becky. "I know it's your office, but could we have a minute?"

"Sure." She looks to me, making sure that I'm okay with her going, and leaves.

As the door clicks shut behind Becky, Seth forces his spine straight and meets my eyes. "We had a fight last night."

The news doesn't shock me, but I shake my head to show that I'm still not understanding.

Not only does Seth break eye contact, but he bends forward, causing his hair to curtain around the sides of his face and help obscure his expression. "It was about you," he says, very, very quietly.

"Me?" Okay… still not shocked. Just trying to figure out what happened. "About me helping you?"

"No, not this time."

"Then… what?"

For a moment, I think he's not going to answer and when he does, I see why he hesitated to say it. "She's gotten it into her head that I'm in love with you."

Chapter Twenty

I blink as the shock finally hits. Simone thinks Seth is in love with me? "Why on Earth would she think that?" I ask him.

"Your guess is probably better than mine," he tells the carpet.

Seth's hair is parted in a straight line down the middle, and I focus on the sliver of scalp it shows. "So, what did you tell her when she said that?"

His scalp pinkens at the question. "That it's none of her business who I do or do not care about."

"Ah," I say. I can see how the lack of denial would set her off. But, still... "Simone believes what she wants to believe. There probably wasn't anything you could have said to make things better. You know, short of swearing undying devotion to her."

"I never wanted you in the middle of this, but I dragged you there anyway. I'm sorry."

My urge is to hug him, but I stay put. "You didn't drag me. I walked in."

He shakes his head. "I should never have asked you to help me."

"You shouldn't have had to."

His body goes still.

I'm going to say something else, though I'm not sure what, but Becky saves me with a rapid knock followed by the door opening and an announcement that it's time to go next door.

We take the short walk to Mr. Atherton's office and find Simone sitting on the nearside of the principal's desk, her head held high and her shoulders straight. She doesn't look at me as I come in and take on the chairs lined up against the back wall. A plump, short, little woman stands to the side of the room. She gives me a gentle smile as my eyes take in the brooch she's wearing. It's a symbol used by sorcerers to mark themselves as licensed magic users. I know just enough about sorcerers to know that's the right word for this woman and that the word "sorceress" is considered sexist.

Principal Atherton types something on his computer, then turns his attention to Simone as Becky closes the door.

"Miss Rutherford," the werewolf says coldly. "Do you know why you're here?"

"I have no idea." The response is fluid and confident.

"So you haven't seen this?" he asks, pushing a piece of paper toward her.

She glances at the printout. I can't see it from my viewpoint, but I'm pretty sure I know what it's of. Simone snorts. "The whole school's seen it."

"And..." Mr. Atherton leads.

Simone's head cocks to the side, and I can imagine the smirk she undoubtedly wears. "And I have no idea what it has to do with me."

"So you're saying that you had nothing to do with the creation or distribution of this image?" He taps the paper with one hand while staring intently at Simone.

"Of course it wasn't me. I don't know why you'd even suspect me."

"I see." Mr. Atherton leans back, his gaze still intent on his prey. "So you have no objections to allowing Ms. Ravenwing to cast a truth spell on you? Because you have nothing to hide from us?"

She doesn't so much as squirm. "Naturally."

Although I've known about sorcerers my entire life, this is the first time I've seen one in action. I expect candles and incense. What I get is a quickly drawn pattern in the air. A flash of light is the only thing to indicate that Ms. Ravenwing isn't just scribbling imaginary shapes.

"You're good to go," the sorcerer says to Mr. Atherton. "I believe you know how this works. She must answer each question fully, not just with 'yes' or 'no' for the spell to work. If she's lying, she won't be able to finish the sentence."

"I remember," Simone says sullenly. I wasn't there, but I assume this is the same thing she went through after the barn painting incident.

Mr. Atherton homes in on Simone. "Did you take this picture?"

"No, I did not take that picture."

He nods like he'd expected that answer. "Did you create this graphic?"

"No, I did not create this graphic."

Another nod. For my part, I'm trying to remember to breathe. Beside me, Seth places his hand over mine, trying to help me stay calm. Or maybe trying to keep himself calm.

"Did you send an email with this graphic attached?"

I struggle to swallow the lump in my throat as Simone pauses.

"No," she says after a moment. "I sent no emails with this graphic."

"Did you otherwise distribute it?" Mr. Atherton asks quickly.

"No, I did not distribute this graphic." There's a hint of victory in her voice that keeps me from feeling relieved by this answer. Seth's grip tightens. He must hear that note too.

Mr. Atherton leans back and studies Simone for a moment. "Do you know who did distribute this image?"

"No," she says.

The principal's eyebrows go up as he straightens his back. "You know how this goes. Say the whole thing. Do you know who sent this message to the student body?"

"No. I do not know who-" She cuts off dead and grabs at her chest like she's having trouble breathing.

"You may want to change your answer," Mr. Atherton says in a cold voice I would never want directed at me.

I weave my fingers through Seth's and squeeze hard, grateful for the contact. My other hand clutches at my chair, digging into the cushioning around the metal bar of the armrest. It may not surprise me that Simone is behind the picture, but it still breaks my heart and brings tears to my eyes.

"I didn't do it!" Simone gasps.

"And I believe you," Mr. Atherton says without much sympathy. "But I think you know who did."

She shakes her head but doesn't deny it in words.

Mr. Atherton turns his attention to the sorcerer. "Do you have any suggestions, Ms. Ravenwing?"

"I could do a memory extraction," she says after a moment of thought. "Go backwards from here until I hit on something about the picture. How draining it will be for her depends on how far back I'd have to go."

Simone stares at her. "You can't do that!"

The woman's face moves into a pleasant smile. "I assure you I can."

"But..." Finally, Simone deigns to look at me. The pleading in her eyes makes my heart wrench painfully. Seth runs his thumb along the side of my hand. "I didn't do it, Rina. I swear."

"I know," I say. But I also know she was involved, or this would be over by now.

"Last chance," says Mr. Atherton. "Who sent the email?"

"It wasn't me." Simone turns her wide eyes back to the principal. "Why do you think it was me?"

"I'm sure you remember that you're on probation," Mr. Atherton says.

"Y-yes." Her voice catches like she's on the verge of tears.

"If you tell us who did this, you'll get off with detention." He pauses. "And if we have to use Ms. Ravenwing, you'll be expelled."

The word is said without emotion, which makes it all the more harsh. Expulsion. Her parents would kill her for the dishonor. It's amazing she survived the suspension. She's already going to be grounded all summer over that. But she doesn't say anything.

Mr. Atherton turns to the sorcerer, who raises her left hand and begins to trace an outline.

"It was Lyly!" Simone exclaims.

Ms. Ravenwing lowers her hand.

In the hallway, the bell rings to announce classes are about to start.

"Thank you, Simone," says Mr. Atherton. He turns his eyes to me and Seth. "Rina, do you have an objection to what I offered Simone?"

I shake my head mutely.

"Alright." The principal smiles sadly. "In that case, you should probably get to class."

Still without speaking, Seth and I get up. He's still holding my hand as we approach the door, but he drops it so we can walk through. Becky trails behind us. "Are you okay with going to class? Or do you need me?"

"Class is fine," I mumble, starting down the hall. I'll have to go upstairs and get my books. I'm probably going to be late...

"Let me write you guys passes real fast," Becky says. She goes into her office while I stop and wait with Seth.

"You sure you're alright?" he asks. His fingers move a chunk of hair from the side of my face, brushing it behind my ear.

"Yeah."

We take our passes, and I rush away up the stairs so I can sprint to my room for my books. I pause a moment look at myself in the mirror. My eyes seem dead, and my cheeks are even more pale than usual. I run a brush through my hair and waste a few seconds putting on some blush in the hopes it will make me look more alive.

I take my time walking to English. No one passes me on the way since everyone's already in class, and I start to dread having to walk across the room in front of everybody. But what's the alternative? If I don't go to class, I can go find Becky and she'll make sure it's an excused absence. But everyone will know I'm hiding. I'm not going to do that.

So I swallow my trepidation and force myself to turn the knob on the door to the classroom.

Lunch is tense, but other than a lot of glaring across the room, no one does anything to cause a scene. By dinner, Lyly is gone: suspended and picked up by her parents. Simone shows up, but sits alone and keeps her eyes on her food. In all honesty, part of me feels bad for her. If she knew what Lyly was doing and didn't stop her, that's not any worse than my lack of preventing the barn painting. If she didn't know until later, then she's not guilty at all. On the other hand, she may have been sitting next to Lyly and egging her on, in which case she's getting off on a technicality. There's no way for me to know without talking to her, and I'm just not willing to do that.

As the week moves on, people continue to talk about me. I know this because they fall silent as soon as I walk into a room. What I don't know is exactly what they're saying. Even though I try to eavesdrop a few times, it turns out that my spy skills are sadly lacking.

My time is spent focused on training with Seth and helping Troy in the library. I fall further behind in my classes, but figure there'll be time to catch up after the Challenge. Any work I tried to do now would be hopelessly sloppy anyway.

The night before the full moon, I hardly sleep. I'm scared for Seth, and I'm anxious about spending two hours in a car with Simone. But not riding in Eileen's car would mean explaining to her what's been going on between me and her daughter, which I'm still not eager to do. She's going to know something's up, though. It's not like she's an idiot.

Unable to sleep, I go to my computer at five in the morning, I log into Chibifae for the first time in weeks and look for my cousin. Luckily, she's online.

"What are you doing up at this hour?" she types to me in Russian.

"Seth's Challenge is tomorrow," I type back. Although I've been ignoring the game, we've exchanged enough emails for her to know I've been helping him. I haven't told her about anything from the last week, though.

"How's Simone taking it?"

"Don't know. She's not talking to me." I debate telling her about the meme, but decide I'd rather not mention it. I do, however, tell her, "She's been kinda mean to me, actually."

The computer pings as a video chat request comes in from Evgeniya. I accept it and maximize the window, leaving my cute little kitty-fairy standing in her cottage. Like always, Evgeniya looks like she's about to leave for a club. Black streaks stand out in her blonde hair and compliment the grey eyes she received from her father while long, dangly earrings draw out her remarkable cheekbones. Occasionally, people insist we look alike, but I've never seen the resemblance.

"What do you mean, she has been cruel?" she says in English. "Must I fly to America?"

"No, it's not that bad," I tell her, still in Russian. Much like she enjoys the chance to practice her English, I enjoy being able to speak my native tongue, even if it does feel foreign these days.

She stares at me through the monitor, not looking much like she believes me. "Tell me what she has done."

I let out a long breath, then launch into the story.

Evgeniya moves her head to side to side as I finish, a sign that she's processing my words. After a moment, she stills. "You should poison her. Or at least tell her mother."

"I don't want to drag Eileen into this."

"Eileen is already in this," Evgeniya declares. "She should not be allowing her daughter to behave this way."

"I guess," I mumble. "But I don't want to tell her."

"Then ride to the Assembly with Seth. When Eileen asks Simone why you are not with them, Simone will have to explain."

I shake my head. "She'll claim innocence and say that if I was a real friend I'd believe her."

"Still. It would be a more pleasant ride."

She has a point there, I have to admit. I'm still pondering the issue after I've signed off, meditated, and dressed myself for the day. All that's left to do is eat breakfast and wait.

Chapter Twenty-One

Like usual, I have breakfast with the wolves, who are going to take advantage of the day off to get in some extra time on the slopes. Troy appears to be using the day to get some extra sleep. As I'm finishing my eggs, the others at my table lower their eating utensils to stare at something behind me. I likewise put down my fork, then look over my shoulder to see Simone striding toward my table.

She glares down her nose at me. "You think you're coming to the Meet, don't you?"

"Yes," I answer slowly. "I plan to."

"Well, you're not." She plops a hand on her hip. "Daddy says so."

In addition to having a general invitation to all Meets, an announcement went out about this one saying we were all required to come. "He hasn't told me that."

"Call him. See what he says."

She smirks as I pull out my phone. But I put it down on the table without dialing. "If he didn't want me to come, he would have called me."

"I'm just warning you," she says, as though doing me a favor. "I don't want you to be surprised when Mom doesn't let you in the car."

My eyes follow her as she sashays off.

"Smells rotten," Penny says.

"Indeed." I turn back to my friends. "I'm going to ask the Daes if I can ride with them though."

"Probably a good idea," Madison says before changing the subject to hockey. I don't generally care about sports, but predicting the winner of the Stanley Cup is better than dwelling on Simone.

Amber doesn't seem surprised when I approach her and ask if she thinks I can ride with her, and Seth smiles at me like I was expected when I show up. Even their dad doesn't seem to think it's odd that I'm suddenly tagging along with them.

Maybe Mr. Dae has too much to think about to bother wondering about me. He says very little on the two hour drive. Likewise, the twins are near silent. Seth hums along with the radio, but stares out the window like he's nowhere near the rest of us, and Amber has her head stuck in a copy of *The Scarlet Letter*. I assume it's an English assignment because she usually reads pulp romances.

If I tried to read, I'd get carsick, and I don't feel up to carrying a conversation, so I look out at the landscape and listen to Mr. Dae's MP3 collection. It's playing a Beatles song when my phone buzzes in my pocket. I take it out and look at the display. The caller ID says, "Eileen Rutherford."

My finger hovers over the answer icon. Then it moves to the reject option. Then back to answer... I take a breath and press down. "Hey, Eileen."

"Why aren't you in the car with your family, daughter?"

The direct question is not one I welcome, but at least she didn't start out yelling at me like I expected. She doesn't sound angry at all, but tired. Which is how I feel too. I lean back in my seat.

After I fail to answer immediately, Eileen goes on. "When you didn't answer my email, I assumed you didn't want to come at all. Not that you were taking sides against your sister, my daughter."

"Email?" I haven't received an email from her in weeks.

"At least your phone is fixed. Or did you get a new one?"

"My phone's fine."

"Ah," she says. There's a pause. "It was always fine, wasn't it?"

"Yeah…"

"Alright. I think I see what's happening."

"That makes one of us."

She sighs audibly. "I think that my younger two daughters are both disappointing me today. But you are still my daughters. You understand?"

"Yeah. I love you, too."

"Good-bye, daughter. I'll see you at the Meet?"

"See you there."

I hang up and stare at the scenery in confusion. How many times did she call me "daughter" in that conversation? She's done it before, but it seemed like she was trying to drill it into my head. Maybe she's afraid that if the treaty between her family and Seth's is broken, the treaty between her family and mine will fall apart as well, so she's reminding me we have a connection.

The word lingers in my head the rest of the drive and pings loudly when we pull up into the empty lot by the barn our Meets are held in. I'm almost certain there was more to that word than is obvious, but I can't figure out what.

My legs ache when I get out of the SUV, and I stumble through my first few steps, prompting Seth to grab my elbow. His breath is warm against my cheek as he bends to whisper, "You okay, kitten? You don't have to do this."

His eyes are pinched with worry. He's about to face someone he has almost no chance against, and he's worried about me? "I'm fine."

I straighten my shoulders and continue toward the barn. Amber's expression seems thoughtful as she twists the strap of the messenger bag she wears and falls in on the side of me opposite her brother.

The twins' mother waits by the door, looking just as unflappable as ever. We were told earlier that she came in with a friend to help set up for the Meet. She holds out her arms to hug her children with genuine affection, and then pulls both of their faces down so that she can kiss their cheeks. She links her arms through theirs as she smiles at me.

"Katerina," she says. "It means a lot to see you here with Seth. Thank you."

Despite the cold, my skin heats up.

The elder Daes walk inside first, trailed by Seth, with me and Amber taking up the rear. Usually, there's a ton of chatter before a Meet, but the room is ominously silent even before we enter. Also unlike usual, almost everyone I see has dressed up. There are several suits and no jeans other than mine and Seth's. Oddly enough, Seth's relative informality makes him seem not shabby, but confident. The looseness in his stroll shows no signs of nerves, and I can't help but wonder if he's really as relaxed as he seems.

My group makes its way to the front of the completely silent room.

I hesitate when we get there. There are four seats under the Clowder Dae banner and five under Rutherford's. I'm clearly meant to sit there, but I can't handle the thought of sitting next to Simone right now. Maybe I'll just sit on the end and hope she sits on the opposite one.

Seeing my indecision, an elder by the name of Moira Kurtman waves me to a seat previously occupied by her purse on the end of a Clowder Dae row. I take it gratefully. Ms. Kurtman is one of the few elders sympathetic to Seth, so I approach her as though she's a haven. She pats my knee as I sit down and offers me a breath mint from a tin she has out.

I take the mint for something to focus on as, around me, people slowly start to speak quietly to one another.

"So, you've sided with the boy?" Ms. Kurtman asks. Her eyes are on Seth, who sits casually leafing through what I suspect is a copy of the engagement contract. He has to have the thing memorized by now; I nearly do.

"I think it's best for both of them," I say, watching Seth. He flicks a few pages backward to reread something, then glances up at me before whispering something to Amber. Her eyes widen and zip my way.

"And what about you?" Ms. Kurtman asks.

I stop watching the twins and look at the woman beside me. Despite the title of "elder" she's actually not any older than my parents, and she's much more approachable than my uptight mother has ever been. "What's best for me?"

She nods, but doesn't clarify the question.

"It doesn't have anything to do with me."

Her mouth twitches toward a smile. "Nothing to do with you? Your adopted father entered the agreement with the Dae Clowder minutes after claiming you. It seems to me, you're right in the middle of it."

Squinting at her doesn't make her words any more clear, and before I can beg for clarification, the door swings open and Dan struts into the barn, looking big and intimidating. The silence returns abruptly and accompanies him and the other Rutherfords on their march to the front.

As his family sits, Dan turns my way with a frown. "I would have all three of my daughters with me."

My stomach flips as everyone in the room looks at me.

"Best go," Ms. Kurtman whispers.

I force myself to stand, feeling like a newborn fawn with legs too wobbly to be of use. Behind Dan, the twins are pointing at something on the papers and nodding with excitement.

And it hits me. My name isn't Rutherford, but I'm Dan's daughter. And my birthday is three months after Simone's, so I'm the younger daughter. And the contract is clear: the engagement is between Seth and the younger daughter. He's not supposed to be betrothed to Simone, but to me.

Our eyes meet, and I know he's figured out the same thing.

Chapter Twenty-Two

My knees aren't shaking as I walk to my new seat, but it wouldn't take much to make them. My stomach churns like crazy, making me happy we haven't had dinner yet. After I sit, I meet Seth's eyes and get the distinct impression he's trying to tell me something. Unfortunately, I don't possess an ounce of telepathy. I'm not even completely sure what the look Simone gives me means, although I have more of a clue about that.

Dan looks out over the gathering. "Before we address the Challenge, is there any other business for us to consider?"

There's always other business at Meets and even though I silently pray that people will just let us get on with the fight, this one isn't an exception. As Sanjay Dutt launches into a complaint he's made a dozen times already, I tune out and try to come up with a battle strategy. Because there will still be a battle. While I'd like to think Seth would prefer being engaged to me over being engaged to Simone, neither of us want an arranged marriage. Although if I were going to have one... I shake my head. No good can come from a thought that starts like that. There will be a battle. The only thing that's changed is that now I have the right to join on Seth's side, if I have the guts.

My instinct to breathe barely overcomes my desire to fade out of existence as the Meet proceeds. Minutes drag on, each one impossibly long. Simone sits beside me, radiating hostility, and Seth keeps looking at me. I feel stupid for not knowing what he's trying to communicate, even though there's no way I could know. My teeth hold my lower lip in place while I struggle to look calm and collected.

Dan concludes the other business at long last, then proclaims, "And now, the Challenge. Seth Dae?"

Seth stands slowly, his eyes roaming rapidly and without focus. I know he's rehearsed what he's supposed to say, but he looks lost.

I shoot to my feet. "As the subjects of the agreement, we, Seth Carrollton Dae and Katerina Ramonova Andreyushkina, hereby officially Challenge our marriage contract."

Dear God... I try not to tremble as everyone once again stares at me.

"Excuse me?" says Simone. "You have no marriage contract."

"Yes, I do." I'm shaking, but it doesn't keep me from speaking. "I am the youngest daughter of Clowder Leader Rutherford."

Our eyes meet and tears appear in Simone's as she shakes her head. "No, you're not. I am. It's my marriage contract, and I do not Challenge it."

Dan clears his throat. "The Challenge has been heard."

"What?" Simone jumps to her feet. "Dad!"

Her father narrows a glare on her. No one can glare quite like Dan Rutherford. It's effective even against someone as stubborn as Simone, who sits down begrudgingly. Nicole leans around her sister to give me a smile and a thumbs-up.

As both parties are in agreement, Dan could allow the Challenge to go uncontested, but the set of his jaw tells me he'll do no such thing. He might be willing to go along with me being the subject of the agreement rather than Simone, but that doesn't mean he wants the agreement disregarded.

Across the stand, Mr. Dae rises. "Clowder Dae does not contest the Challenge. We believe in the right to select one's own mate."

My eyes widen at the second sentence. The first one was expected, but the script would have had him omit the next bit.

Dan doesn't comment on the matter, but simply states, "Clowder Rutherford contests the Challenge. The matter will be settled at moonrise."

This prompts our audience to stand and shuffle toward the door. Dan turns to me as they go and gives me a nod that manages to convey that while he's not letting me have my way, he is proud of me.

On impulse, I rush up to Dan and wrap my arms around him. I rise to my toes as he hugs me back, and I whisper, "We're going to kick your rear end, old man."

He ruffles my hair. "I'll be disappointed if you don't. It's two to one."

I flinch as Simone demands, "How is this happening?"

Dan lets go of me and turns to deal with his daughter, a conversation I simply refuse to be a part of. Without regret, I cross to the Daes. Seth won't meet my eyes, but Amber wraps me in an enormous hug.

"No celebrating yet," I remind her. "We still have the actual Challenge."

We may have a two-to-one advantage, but I'm far from certain that's going to be enough. Dan is good, and he's not going to go easy on us.

"Simone looks like she's going to explode," Amber says as we start toward the door. Seth walks in front of us, his back tense now. Amber sounds amused, but I can't find humor in Simone's pain. I never wanted to hurt her, let alone torture her in front of the entire snow leopard community. I'd try to calm her down if I thought it would do any good.

I'd love to know why Seth is acting so uptight all of a sudden. It's almost like he doesn't want to be doing this. I stumble at the thought. Maybe he doesn't. Maybe he didn't object to being engaged, just to his fiancée.

My pace increases until I'm beside him, and I reach out to put a hand on his arm. "You okay?"

"Yeah." He smiles for me, but it doesn't touch his eyes. They're… haunted.

"Are you having second thoughts?" I whisper as quietly as I can.

He looks at me for a moment. "Are you?"

"No."

He tries to smile again. "Then no."

I don't believe him, but there's no time to talk about it. The pressure of the moon is already strong, and growing stronger by the heartbeat. It seeps into my bones and makes me vibrate with familiar anticipation.

As the press of the moon becomes something impossible to ignore, a circle forms in the clearing behind the barn. I force myself to walk calmly to the center of it, and Seth paces me perfectly. His heat radiates against the side of my body, and although I know there are a million other scents here, he's all I can smell. It may or may not be a good idea, but I grab his hand and give it a squeeze. The contact relaxes me and makes Seth's posture ease just a hair, enough that he no longer looks painfully tense. He squeezes back and a sense of rightness overcomes me. It's right that we're doing this together.

When he lets go of my hand, I subdue a shiver and turn the motion into a stretch instead. I arch my back until it pops and the transformation takes over. Seth is much larger in cat-form than I am. My back comes up only slightly past his belly. But even bigger looms Dan Rutherford. Although he was my first trainer in human-form, I've never faced off with him as a cat.

Seth rubs his shoulder against mine before dropping into a defensive stance that I copy. I wish we'd spent more time sparring last moon, but it's too late for thoughts like that.

Dan sits, waiting for us to make the first move. How long is he willing to wait? Holding this stance is going to tire me eventually.

Without warning, Seth leaps. I'm only a second behind him, and as Dan rebuffs Seth's attack, I land on Dan's back. I dig my nails in deep, and though Dan is quick to dislodge me, I leave a row of thin gouges.

While I recover from being thrown, Seth circles until we're on opposite sides of Dan. Considering Seth the larger threat, Dan turns to stay facing him. As if we'd rehearsed it, Seth and I spring at the same time. He gets clobbered back, but I sink my teeth into Dan's shoulder. As blood fills my mouth, I move my head to make the wound worse, excited to be ripping into my prey.

As Dan aims his massive paw at my face, Seth attacks his good shoulder, which quickly becomes as bloody as the one I bit. My vision spins at the impact, and I roll sideways in the snow.

We back off, sides heaving. Dan's winded and hurt, but still has plenty of fight left in him, and it's still possible he'll get to us despite our initial success. In fact, the next time we back off of him, we're both bleeding nearly as much as he is.

Seth and I look at each other, careful to keep Dan in sight as well. Our lack of telepathic abilities doesn't stop us from moving forward in timed unison, or from coordinating a series of attacks that ultimately win out.

Bloody, wobbly, and completely out of breath, Dan lowers his head in concession.

My legs give out under me, and I crash onto the snow. With a thump, Seth collapses beside me, and we struggle to breathe as Dan limps away. A mass of fur collects around us, but all I see before me are Seth's eyes. So blue... So tired.

People still in human form tend to our wounds, each sting bringing me more into the moment. The numbness that took over once combat started fades, leaving behind pain and more pain.

I'm relieved when the first aid is over, and I'm left to my quiet suffering. I drag myself close to Seth and fall asleep with my flank touching his.

When I wake, it's past dawn and close to moonset. Seth is awake, licking his paw like nothing interesting has happened recently. Amber is curled up between her mom and dad, and we're completely surrounded by their Clowder. I don't know where any of the Rutherfords are. A worry seeps into my mind. I haven't seen the Clowders so segregated in years. Was the marriage contract really all that was holding us together?

Chapter Twenty-Three

"Katerina!"

My head snaps toward the sound of Dan's voice as I sit in a folding chair by the Daes' SUV. The motion nearly drips syrup off the plate of pancakes provided by Mr. Dae's portable hot plate. My foster father walks up to me with a slight limp. His cheek is marred by a long scratch, and I try to remember if it was me or Seth who gave it to him.

"Daughter," he says in poorly-accented Russian. "Why are you here?"

Um... I look at him, unable to think of anything to say.

He lets out a sigh, and when he speaks again, it's in English. "You are the one who severed our tie to Clowder Dae."

"Oh, please." It's Seth's mom who speaks. She's a foot shorter than Dan is and weighs much less, but she stands up in front of my foster father and somehow gives the impression that she's looking down at him. "Come on, Danny. It was mutually resolved, and it triggers a renegotiation, not a war."

"Really, Anna?" says Dan, who I have never before heard referred to as *Danny*. His expression softens as he regards Ms. Dae, but his posture remains rigid. "And you're that certain that we can renegotiate a peace? Don't you remember how hard this one was?"

"Of course I do." Anna Dae folds her arms crossly. "Why else would I have sold my son's future? But now that we have had peace, I don't think it will be too easily discarded."

"Well, I hope you're right."

Mr. Dae puts his hand on his wife's shoulder. "You know as well as I do that she's always right."

The corner of Dan's mouth ticks. "I know you'd say that. Still not so sure I do."

Amber and I trade a confused look. What are they talking about?

Ms. Dae clicks her tongue. "Don't let Eileen hear you saying that."

"She's said worse to me," he says, but doesn't seem bothered by it. "But, at any rate, I don't think I can let you keep my daughter."

"No one kidnapped me," I interrupt. "I asked them for a ride is all."

My foster father raises his eyebrows at me. "You're not that naive."

And I can't really argue, because I knew showing up with the Daes said something yesterday. I guess being with them now is saying something too. But, like yesterday, it's something I want to say. "You're right. And I mean what I'm saying being here. We're all still friends, Dad. At least we should be."

His face softens. That's the first time I've ever called him "Dad." Even "Dan" was an advancement; he was "Mr. Rutherford" for the first few years I was with his family. He nods slowly. "Alright. I'll let you make your statement."

I put down my food so I can give him a hug. "Thank you."

He grunts, makes his goodbyes, and leaves me with the Daes. Which is when I realize I never actually asked for a ride home... what if they were planning on taking their kids to their house for the weekend? School is between where we are and their house though, so hopefully they don't mind stopping.

"We'll get you back to school," Mr. Dae says before taking a sip of the coffee in this hand. "We were taking the kids back anyway. And I like your statement."

After everyone has finished breakfast, we get on the road quickly. This time Ms. Dae rides with us, and I suspect it's because they're going to have a long conversation after they drop us off.

A long conversation is probably what I need to have with my parents, but with the time difference, it's too late by the time we get back to school. It's a blessing, really. I'd much rather write to them about everything that just happened than to tell them on the phone.

After a shower, I get out my laptop and spend over an hour trying to compose an email that makes sense and doesn't sound like I just threw away the only thing keeping Alaska from breaking out into civil war again. I'm still not happy with it when I'm interrupted by a knock on the door.

"Hey!" Amber sticks her head into the room after I call out a greeting. "Perchance, could you do me a favor?"

"Maybe..."

Amber smiles, looking radiant, and walks inside. "Good answer. Could you do something about Seth?"

I close my laptop and move it to the side. "What do you mean?"

"He's..." She draws in a breath. "He's upset about something, but he won't tell me what."

That doesn't sound good, but if he won't tell her... "Why would he tell me?"

"Because you're not his sister?" she offers. "I can't so much as breathe without him glaring at me today. He would never be so ungracious to you."

"Maybe."

I don't know what I can do, but I go find him anyway. He's in the music room, sitting at an upright piano playing a melancholy song. The music is sad enough I grow almost teary-eyed just hearing it, but I enter into the room anyway and stand behind Seth as he plays. His hair is loose, flowing down his back like the notes flow from his instrument.

He replays a piece, then jots something down on a piece of paper. I stand still, knowing that if I don't make any noise he'll never know I'm here. And for a good five minutes, he doesn't. But then, for some reason, he looks behind him.

Caught watching, I walk forward and try to act like I just got here. I take a seat on the fluffy red sofa that sits against the wall beside the piano. "Am I bothering you?"

"No." He plays another series of notes, one that's not any more cheerful than the ones that came before. "This isn't finished. Do you have any requests?"

"Something happier?" I ask. "I mean, we're supposed to be happy, aren't we?"

He smiles faintly. "I was never very good at *supposed*."

A frown takes over my face as his fingers play something jaunty. I let him go through the entire piece even though I can tell his heart isn't in it. He finishes and sits staring at the keyboard.

"What's wrong?" I ask.

He shakes his head.

I inch to the edge of the couch, my hands grasping the front of the cushion under me. "You're worrying me, Seth."

"I'm fine," he says, but his eyes are pinched and his voice is off somehow. Standing, he runs his hands through his hair and chuckles without mirth. "My ego's just a little bruised. I'll get over it."

"Bruised ego?" I tilt my head in question. "Why? We won."

He laughs again, not sounding any happier than before. "Yeah. Well."

A suspicion hits me and makes me frown. "Is it because you needed help? From me?"

"No," he answers quickly. "I thought we worked really well together."

"We did."

I watch him watching the floor and can't for the life of me imagine what he's thinking. On the wall, the clock clicks the seconds as they pass.

"I..." he starts to speak, but trails off immediately.

"You...?"

His eyes squeeze shut. "Did you hesitate at all?"

About what? "Huh?"

He shakes his head. "Nothing. Never mind."

"Did I hesitate about what?" More seconds tick by as he steadies his breath. I get up and take his hand. "What are you asking?"

His fingers wrap around mine. "Sometimes," he whispers. Just the one word.

"Sometimes what?"

He drags his eyes from our clasped hands up to my face. "Are you playing games?"

I drop his hand and take a step back, which makes him sigh and collapse onto the couch. He sits, looking up at me with an unreadable expression. "You told me you like girls."

There's an implied question in the statement. "I do."

"And yet..." He pauses for a moment. "And yet, sometimes it seems like there's something between us."

And now that it's been said, it's obvious. "There is."

"What?" he asks softly.

"I don't know. But I think it's important." I sit down beside him, and we move in unison to join our hands between us. His fingers tremble as they clutch at me.

"I want to kiss you."

What a lovely idea. "Then I think you should."

"I'm scared to," he whispers, although he leans toward me like he's going to do it anyway.

"Why?" I whisper back, arching toward him.

He closes his eyes and draws closer. "Because I don't want to lose you."

Our lips are so close I can feel his breath on mine, but there's a wall between us. "Why would you lose me?"

He moves back as his eyes slide open, then he gives me a rueful smile. "That's what happens when I kiss girls. They realize I'm not that interesting after all."

My heart cracks. "Maybe you've been kissing the wrong girls."

"Maybe..." His eyes are locked on my lips; I can almost feel them.

I shove past the metaphorical wall between us to press my mouth to his. And as he pulls me tight against his chest, I know for a fact that he was kissing the wrong girls before.

Chapter Twenty-Four

We separate slowly, eyes locked together.

"Well..." Seth says. "You're not laughing. And you're not running away."

"Running away? You've got to be joking."

He frowns. "I don't speak Russian."

Now, I do laugh. His kiss knocked me back to my native language, and he thinks I'm going to run away? I wrap one hand around the back of his neck and use the other to push back his hair. "I said that I'm not going anywhere."

"But you are laughing." He leans his cheek against my palm, his eyes searching mine.

"Because I'm happy!"

"I can live with that," he says, just before kissing me again.

A sound from the hallway pulls us apart. It's just someone walking toward us, and probably someone who would just walk past. Yet we put several painful inches between us, agreeing without talking about it that we want to keep whatever is between us as solely our business. At least, I think we're agreeing about that. The only other alternative I can think of is that he'd be embarrassed to be seen kissing me, and the thought of that makes me feel ill.

He puts his hand over mine and runs his thumb along the side of mine. "I thought I was going crazy," he whispers.

"I'm sorry." I bend my head forward, letting my hair partially mask my cheeks. "I should have told you I was bi, not a lesbian. It just seemed like a weird thing to bring up."

"I could have asked," he says. "But it seemed like a weird thing to bring up."

I smile. "I'm glad we sorted it out, though."

"Me too."

He gives me a look like he's going to kiss me another time, but the person in the hallway stops at the door.

"Seth?" It's Michaela, and she rushes into the room once she spots us. Her brown hair is mussed and her eyes are frantic.

His thumb stops rubbing against mine, but his hand stays put as he frowns at his friend in concern. "What is it?"

She stops in front of us. Her eyes land on me for a heartbeat before she dismisses my presence and looks only at Seth. "You remember how I had that dream when Aliah was hurt? The one that let us find her?"

"Of course."

"I had another one."

Seth squeezes my hand. "Aliah again?"

"No." Michaela looks at me for another second before turning her attention back to Seth. "Promise not to tell Warren?"

"I thought you accepted him as your life mate," Seth says, his eyes narrowing. "I'm pretty sure that means no secrets. And I'm certain he thinks it means that."

"Save the lecture." She draws a breath. "I'll tell him. Eventually. But you don't."

"Alright."

We both watch her as she says nothing for several seconds. Then she blurts, "It's Troy."

I jerk back in surprise. I'd heard that Michaela had some kind of ability to sense danger in people who are close to her, but I didn't realize Troy still counted. I can see why she wouldn't want Warren knowing that.

Seth's voice is cautious as he asks, "And you're sure it was a vision, not just your imagination?"

There's a hint of tears in her eyes as she shakes her head. "No. But I can't find him."

At this point, they both look at me. "I'll send Penny a text and see if he went snowboarding with them. He's supposed to be confined to the building, but maybe he decided to break out anyway." A quick message is sent, and then we sit here and wait in an awkward silence. Seth clutches my hand again, and the moments slide by.

After a few moments, Michaela's eyes suddenly widen, focused on Seth's hand. She looks from our hands to his face, an open question on her features.

Seth looks impassively back, not giving away anything, but not moving his hand away either. I'm fairly certain she's one of those wrong girls he kissed, but I don't know if she laughed or ran. And I don't know how he felt about it when she did.

The notion that I'm just something to make her jealous strikes and almost makes me move my hand. But before I can, they're both grinning.

Michaela folds her legs under her and gracefully plops onto the floor. "Let's pretend we've never met," she tells me. She waves. "Hi. I'm Mike."

"Rina," I respond, uncomfortable now that I'm reminded she has every reason to dislike me. "And I'm sorry."

"Sorry?" Her head cocks to the side. "For having bad taste in friends? It's improving, so I'll forgive you."

I try to smile at her. "I should have done more to rein in Simone."

"Kitten," says Seth, "she never listened to either of us. And Mike knows that."

"Yes, indeed." Michaela nods. "Simone doesn't care about anyone's opinion but Simone's. And as I hear it, she's been pretty crappy to you lately."

"It's kinda mutual," I say, glancing at Seth. I mean, from Simone's point of view, I did just finish swiping her fiancé. And to add insult to injury, I didn't even stay engaged to him. Although I may be dating him. Maybe. I should ask him, but don't want to do it with Michaela here.

"No, it's not." Seth scoots closer and puts his arm around me. "You've never done anything just because it would hurt her."

"That doesn't mean I haven't hurt her."

My phone beeps before anyone can offer an opinion on that. My heart sinks as I read the response. "He's not snowboarding."

Michaela curses. "He's in trouble."

"We don't know that yet," Seth says calmly. He quickly squeezes my shoulders, then lets go so he can stand up. He holds his hand down to help me up, which I don't need but appreciate anyway. "Where have you checked?"

"Everywhere."

Seth frowns in thought, and looks at me. "He's your friend. Where would he be?"

"You're sure he wasn't in his room?" I ask Michaela. "You actually went in? He might not have answered the door if he didn't feel like it."

"No," she says slowly. "But I yelled through the door that it was me."

Then he should have answered… if he heard her. "Maybe he was in the shower or something."

Since we're right beside it, we give the library a complete go over, with no luck, before we go upstairs. No one seems too surprised when Troy's room is definitely empty.

"And your other friends are all snowboarding?" Michaela verifies with me as Seth closes the door.

"Yeah," I say, starting down the hall.

"When's the last time you saw him?" Seth asks the all-were.

"He was for sure in classes Thursday, but I don't remember seeing him after that."

I make a noise of denial. "He was at dinner that night."

"But not breakfast Friday?" Seth says.

"No." There weren't any classes Friday though, because of the full moon, so it didn't set off any alarms. "I figured he slept in."

"Okay." We start down the stairs. "So, we double check all the common rooms, and if we still haven't found him, we tell Atherton."

"Atherton's not here," Michaela says.

"Not here on a full moon?" Seth sounds as incredulous as I feel. Mr. Atherton has vanished during other moons, but only when something really important is going on elsewhere. Otherwise, he's here to make sure we behave ourselves despite our animals being so close to the surface. "Where is he?"

"I'm not sure. Rumor is he's mediating something for your lot."

Seth and I trade a glance, and I ask, "That's good, right? That they're negotiating the new treaty already."

"Probably," he confirms slowly.

Michaela frowns in confusion. "New treaty? But I thought you just changed fiancées. Why would that change the treaty?"

My eyes go to Seth, in case he wants to field the question. The way he stares at the carpet tells me he doesn't though. "We realized the contract applied to me, yes."

Seth is really getting into his study of the flooring, but he moves to grab my hand and finishes the thought for me. "But we Challenged anyway."

"Why?" Michaela blurts. Her cheeks flare red, and her hand twitches like she wants to cover her mouth. "Sorry. I mean, okay… It's just… you seem like you're together."

I look to Seth, and his eyes come up to mine. Softly, he states, "We do seem to be."

"Yes," I agree. "But if we're going to be together it's because we want to be, not because other people made a contract."

Seth nods and looks back to his friend. "So we Challenged. Together. And won. Thus the new negotiation."

"Gotcha," Michaela says slowly. "There's a lot of value in choosing to be with someone rather than just going along with someone else's idea."

"Exactly!" I say.

And Michaela screams.

She wobbles, and Seth leaps forward to stabilize her. "Mike?" he asks in a sharp tone. "What's wrong?"

She lets out a whimper before answering, "They're hurting him."

"They who?"

"I can't see them." She pulls herself away from Seth and rakes both hands through her hair. "But he's in a cave. The same one he had Aliah in, I think."

"We need to tell someone." Seth starts toward the staff offices. Someone has to be hanging around being in charge in Mr. Atherton's absence.

"No!" Michaela springs to grab his arm. "Whoever this is, they're hurting an all-were. It's probably the all-were that's been lurking around. No offense, but you normal weres have no chance against people like me. I have to go."

"Not alone you don't."

"Seth." Her voice catches on his name. "I don't want anyone else dying. Definitely not you."

Last time there was an all-were battle around here, one of the wolf pack was killed. It wasn't Michaela's fault, but she clearly feels guilty about it. She and Seth lock eyes with each other, communicating on a level I'll admit to being slightly jealous of.

"No," Michaela says softly. "You stay here."

"No, I don't." He shakes his head. "Whoever this is may be dangerous, but not as dangerous as Warren will be if he finds out I let you go by yourself."

It's a very valid point. There's no fury to match that of a werewolf who thinks you endangered his life mate. Even going with her, Seth could be doomed for letting her go at all. As if he could stop her...

"Fine," she says with a growl in her voice. "I don't have time to argue with you."

She darts to the front door and rushes down the front steps too fast for the ice that's always on them. Between one step and the next, she shimmers, turning herself into a beautiful arctic wolf.

Seth glances at me, his lips parting. I'm certain he's about to tell me to stay, so I cut him off. "If you're going, I'm going. No arguments."

He has the sense not to protest. "Can you shift without the moon?"

If we're going to keep up with Michaela, we're going to have to. I nod, even though I've never tried to change while the moon wasn't out. I tread carefully down the stairs before stopping to try.

My eyes closed, I picture my cat-self, willing my fur to sprout and my body to rearrange itself into the familiar shape. Nothing happens. Beside me, I hear Seth huff and can tell from the sound of it that he is now in cat-form.

I will not be left. That's just not acceptable.

The familiar tingle of transformation seeps across my body, and I stretch out, whipping my tail in triumph. But there's no time to celebrate the milestone I just passed, not with Michaela putting distance between us every second.

Together, Seth and I leap forward to bound after her. The snow flies from our paws as we cut through the chilly afternoon air. By next week, it will be time for the thaw, and all this loveliness will turn to mud, but for today it's glorious. At least until I remember why we're running. My friend is in trouble. Possibly serious trouble. I run faster.

Chapter Twenty-Five

We leap over a rock wall and run down into the gulch hidden behind it, the wind ruffling our fur and bringing the scent of something ominously odd. In addition to the familiar scent of Troy, I smell the odor of a female all-were, but also something I've never smelled before. We slow down, our noses wiggling as we process the unusual scent. It's not a human, a were, or any animal local to these woods. It reminds me a little of the scent of the sorcerer, but it's not that either.

Seth and I come to a gradual stop, but Michaela rushes forward. If she has a plan, I don't know what it is, and I'm not thrilled at the idea of running blind. We look at each other, and Seth huffs at me in question. I meow back, trying to convey that I don't know what to do. Maybe we should change back into our human forms?

I'm considering transforming when Michaela howls in pain, turning my attention to her. Seth and I both sprint to where she rolls in the snow. As we get to her, the shimmer of shapeshifting overtakes her and she takes on her human appearance. She pants in exhaustion and pain as Seth bumps his nose against her shoulder.

"I wasn't trying to change," she gasps. "Something forced it."

Seth glances at me. I feel a slight pressure to shift, but it's the same as it has been since I changed. I'd assumed it was a normal feeling when one changes without the moon. I shake my head and try to shrug my shoulders, even though that's pretty hard to do as a cat.

A rustling sound warns us of someone approaching, sending me into hiding against the cliff face. The snow is firm enough here that with luck I didn't leave any prints. However, I realize with a sinking feeling, I did leave Seth.

I could have sworn he was moving with me, but he's still there with Michaela, crouched beside her. And he's shifted back into human. Maybe I should go back and join them.

Seth looks over, his eyes going across me. He smiles when he doesn't see me, which I assume means he wants me to stay hidden.

A loud crunch proceeds a curse in a man's voice. Shortly thereafter, a heavyset lumberjack type snowshoes into sight. He wears a massive parka, a thick wool hat, and a beard that could house an entire family of squirrels. And he carries a gun.

In my lifetime, I've only seen a few guns, so I have no idea what kind of gun the man has, but it looks wicked, and it's pointed at Seth.

"Two more of you?" he says in an accent I can't place. "I knew that boy was lying. How many of you abominations are there?"

"Abominations?" Seth asks, rising slowly to his feet. "What do you mean?"

"So you are going to act stupid, too? Figures."

"We're just students." Seth keeps his eyes on the gun as he helps Michaela stand up. "Our school is right on the other side of that hill over there."

"Uh-huh." The man smirks. "Just students, who are wandering the woods without coats and who coincidentally screamed in pain when they hit my magic barrier."

"Your what?"

"It's why you changed back to your elven forms."

Elven forms? Elves are a type of faerie, the wingless human-looking ones. But why would he think they're elves?

It doesn't matter. He can think whatever he wants. What I need to do is get the gun away from him without giving him a chance to shoot anyone. But even if I can sneak up behind him, he might pull the trigger should I hit him. And maybe the bullet would fly wild because of the impact, but maybe it would zip straight at Seth.

Below, Seth tries to explain that they aren't fae, but the man isn't buying it. On the plus side, he's debating the issue rather than hurting anybody.

Slowly, I edge along the rocks, making sure to keep quiet. If the cave is nearby, maybe I can find Troy, release him, and have an ally. Or maybe the man isn't alone. I stop, indecisive. I should scout, figure out what we're up against, and go back to school for backup. Yeah, that's what I'm going to do.

I sneak with care and precision along the side of the sharp incline as the man motions my friends to move through the bottom of the valley. I try to balance speed with caution, going as fast as I can without chancing being seen. The smell of Troy and the unknown female all-were intensify, but they do seem to be alone. My pace increases, but unless the others slow down, I'm not going to beat them to the cave by enough time to do anything. That telepathic link I don't have to Seth would be useful round about now.

An oomph sounds through the gulch, the sound of someone falling.

"Get up!" comes the man's voice.

"I think I twisted my ankle," Seth responds.

Good job, Seth!

The more space I put between us, the faster I feel comfortable going, and I'm soon within sight of a wide-mouthed cave. I take a deep breath and plow into it.

Troy sits with his hands bound behind him, whispering to a girl with tears streaming down her cheeks. She's the same girl I saw in the woods weeks ago, but now she's streaked with dirt and her hair is a matted nest.

Swiftly, I shift to human, and run around to start untying Troy's bonds.

"Good to see you," he whispers. "But you need to get out of here before Beardy gets back."

"Trying." I concentrate on the knots, wishing I'd been a Girl Scout and learned about such things as a kid.

It hurts my fingers, but eventually I loosen things up enough to slide the ropes off. He leans forward to start on his feet as I move on to the girl.

"Hey," I whisper. "I'm Rina. We're going to get you out of here, okay?"

Troy releases his feet and jumps over to work on the girl's feet as I struggle with the knots binding her hands. They're tighter than Troy's were, and consequently harder.

The girl sniffles. "My name's Ellora."

"Nice to meet you." With a quiet cheer, I undo the worst knot and manage to wriggle the ropes free of her hands. "Let's run. I'll check the coast. If Beardy's too close, I'll try to distract him so you can get out."

I shift back to my cat form and ease out of the cave. I can't smell the others, but all that tells me is that they're downwind of me. I can hear them though, and they're getting close.

I sprint straight for them.

Seth leans on Michaela's shoulder and limps through the snow. I can't tell if he's faking for sure, but he doesn't look like he's in pain, so I'm guessing he is. Good.

I run by the group, making sure to make as much noise as I can.

As I'd hoped, Beardy's head turns as I barrel by him. With the trees between us, I don't think he can see what I am, but I'm sure he catches on that I'm something big. Bigger than most of the things native around here.

"Hello!" he calls out. "You one of them weres?"

Interesting. If he knows about weres, then I'm really confused as to why he thinks my friends are elves. I shake my thoughts off the subject and focus them on getting that gun away from Seth and Michaela.

I zip across the valley until I'm on the opposite side from the cave and start back slower, more quietly.

"Stop!" The man says. Whether he was talking to me or the others, I don't know, but the sounds of their footfalls halt as I continue to creep. "Was someone else with you?"

"Nope," says Seth. "It's just us."

"You're a crummy liar, kid. Who is it?"

"It's my biology class. We're on a field trip."

A faint shuffling tells me Troy and Ellora are getting closer.

I call out. It's an odd sound, not a roar like a lion, more like a pissed off meow.

And Beardy makes the mistake of turning around.

I dart to the side, making sure he can't focus the gun on me, as behind him Seth leaps, changing form midair to hit the man with massive paws tipped with outstretched claws. He sinks his claws into the man's back, making him scream in pain.

My next noise is a lot happier as I trot up the man's dropped gun and nose it further from him. Michaela bends over to pick it up, then moves to target him. "I've got him, Seth."

After growling in the man's ear, Seth backs off of him as Troy appears to the side.

"First off," say Michaela, "why can some of us not shift?"

Beardy stares silently, but Ellora is able to field the question. "Because his device only affects faerie magic, not were magic."

"Faerie magic?"

Troy smiles. "That what we are. Hybrids. Half fae, half were."

That doesn't sound right. I don't know much about faeries, but I know at least one thing. "Being a faerie isn't contagious."

"Not normally," says Ellora. She shivers and wraps her arms around herself. "But when the fae genes are combined with the were aspects, then some parts of the condition can be spread."

"One of my birth parents was a faerie, and the other was a were," Troy says, sounding proud of this. He grins at me. "I know what I am now. She says we're called therians."

"We are." Ellora gives Michaela a soft look. "You're more of a were. You don't have the longevity or immunity to disease that fae have."

"Fine by me," she says, still looking down the barrel at Beardy. "Why are you trying to capture therians?"

He still doesn't say anything, but luckily Ellora knows the answer to this, too. "He's a yager. A faerie with special hunting skills, including the ability to block other faeries' magic."

She shivers again, prompting Troy to say, "We need to either grow some fur or get inside."

"We can't grow fur until he stops projecting his anti-magic."

We all look at Beardy. He draws a breath and shakes his head. "Nope."

The gun shakes in Michaela's hands. Even if she has it in herself to shoot someone, I doubt very much she'd be willing to do it without someone else's life being in danger.

"Then you better start walking," she says in a voice that only shakes a little.

"Not doing that either."

"He's waiting for someone," Troy says. "He mentioned handing us over to them."

Ellora nods, still shivering. "Not the Court. They don't hire yagers. Probably a private collector."

That doesn't sound good. Seth growls, showing his teeth and causing Beardy to pale. The man doesn't back down though.

"Last chance," says Ellora. "Move it."

Beardy looks into Michaela's eyes and smirks. "No."

Ellora yanks the gun from Michaela and shoots.

Chapter Twenty-Six

Beardy sprawls on the snow, bleeding out in waves of red. He moans and puts a hand on the shoulder where Ellora's bullet hit him as his shooter walks up and levels the gun at his face.

"You turning off your magic?" Ellora asks.

From my point of view, nothing changes, but the three all-weres all loosen up. Troy closes his eyes human and opens them again as a snow leopard while Michaela shivers back into wolf-form and lets out a loud howl. Any werewolf hearing that in the middle of the day is going to come running to find out what's wrong. I just hope that whoever was paying Beardy doesn't come as well.

"Alright." The gun doesn't waver at all as Ellora smiles. "Now, get up and start walking."

His eyes blaze hatred as he rises.

"Turn around. Follow the wolf."

He obeys, but he's wobbly. I'm not sure how well he's going to make it, particularly as getting over the rock wall to leave this gulch will involve climbing.

Seth takes his left, and I take the man's right as we follow slowly behind Michaela. Troy and Ellora take up the rear.

Like I predicted, Beardy balks when we get to the wall. "I cannot go up that."

"You'd rather die here?" Ellora asks, not sounding like she has an opinion on the matter either way.

I leap to the top of the wall and look back as Seth lands beside me.

Grumbling, Beardy starts to climb.

He's bleeding more by the time he makes it over the wall, but our sympathies are limited as we continue the journey toward school.

As we draw closer, I start to wonder what we're doing. Are we really going to lead a potentially dangerous prisoner into a school? That doesn't sound like the sanest idea I've ever heard. I stop and shift into human form just before a gust of freezing wind hits me. I could have timed losing my fur better.

"Guys, we shouldn't be taking him to the school. I mean, should we?"

The others trade looks, and Ellora shrugs. "I'll make him walk wherever you tell me to, but if it isn't close he may pass out."

"Outbuilding," says Seth. He pulls his phone out of his pocket, checks it with a shake of his head, and puts it away again. "I was thinking the Annex. We can hole up there and call in the wolf pack."

But, of course, when we get to the Annex, our phones still show zero coverage.

"Alright," Seth says after we all file into the building on two legs, "who's going and who's staying?"

Troy answers quickly, "Rina and I'll go."

Seth's eyes narrow at him and my eyebrows go up, although neither of us contradict him.

Michaela puts a hand on Seth's arm, pulling his attention to her. "We need a leopard here as a second weapon, and whoever goes should have one too. In case they run into this guy's friends."

"Yes," agrees Ellora. She settles into a chair with the gun pointed squarely at Beardy's chest as he rests at one of the desks. "And, you, keep your hands in view."

Seth looks to me. "You want to stay here or go on?"

I'm not sure which I'd prefer, but I'm better suited to working with Troy than Seth would be, so I say, "I'll go."

He nods, accepting the answer though he does so without cheer. "Be careful. And stay at the school once you get there.

We'll be fine. The wolves are probably on their way already thanks to Michaela's call."

I nod back and shimmer into my cat self.

Seth opens the door for me, and runs his hand through my fur as I go past him. The touch is almost enough to make me stop and refuse to leave him, but I force myself out into the cold. I trot to the school, going slower than I would on my own because Troy isn't used to this form and can't keep up with me. I would suggest he change into something else, but I'm not sure he'd be any more swift in another body. That of a snow leopard is pretty much ideal for crossing snow quickly.

We rush into the main building as soon as we're human again and find Becky in her office. She listens to our story with widening eyes. As soon as we tell her that our friends are in the Annex with a prisoner, she lets out a gasp and leaps from her chair. She pulls her phone from her pocket as she walks to the door, but stops before going into the hallway.

"You two," she growls. "You. Stay. Here."

We nod.

"Promise!"

"We'll stay here," I tell her. "I promise."

She nods tersely and storms out the door. As she retreats, I hear her talking to Mr. Atherton on the phone. She leads with, "You're not going to believe this…"

As her footsteps rapidly fade, I walk to the window and look out at the dimming landscape. It'll be dark soon, and I hope Seth makes it back before then because I have a feeling Beardy's friends were due by sunset.

After a good ten minutes of quiet, Troy comes up softly behind me. "What are you thinking about?"

"Just worrying about the others."

"Mmm." Heat hits my back as he comes to a stop so close we're nearly touching. "Can I tell you something?"

"I guess." I'd move and put more space between us, but he has me trapped between the window, a chair, and the wall. His scent is strong, but too complex for me to place a name on emotions it might hint at.

"I," is all he says before his voice cuts off with a groan. He steps back, giving me room to breathe. "I don't know how to say this."

I turn and find him facing away from me, his hands buried in his hair.

"I," he says again. He stops for a breath, then spins quickly, his hands falling to his sides. "When that freak had me tied up, all I could think about was not seeing you again."

The words come quickly, one right on top of the other. They're almost too fast to catch and part of me wants to pretend I don't understand what he's saying.

"You," he repeats, his eyes boring into mine. "Not Mike, or my parents, or any of our friends. You."

I stare back, my heart clenching as I try to think of what to say. Hiding behind Seth would be too easy. It has to be something about us being just friends, but those words seem so painfully cliché.

He steps closer and my pulse accelerates. My fight-or-flight instincts are kicking in. I don't want to fight, but I can't run. Even if I hadn't promised to stay here, he's between me and the door.

"Troy," I start. But I don't get to say anything else, because before the word fades his mouth is on mine, his lips soft yet demanding. All in all, not a bad kiss, but I only feel it in my lips.

I move my hands up to his shoulders to push him back, but before I can do more than get in position, he's being ripped away.

"You idiot!" Michaela shrieks as she yanks Troy from me. "You can't force yourself on people! They kill you for that here!"

"I wasn't forcing myself on anyone!" he yells back, wrenching out of her grasp. "And what do you care anyway?"

"I saw you!" she answers the first question, ignoring the second.

His eyes narrow on her. "Everyone in this school knows damned well Katrina here would kick my ass all over this room if she didn't want me touching her."

"Yes," Seth says softly from behind him. His voice sounds limp and dead. I look over to him, but he's already turning away. "She's more than capable of defending herself," he says as he starts down the hallway.

I bite my lip, trying not to cry.

"Troy," I say in a shaky voice. "You got off lucky. If you ever touch me without asking again, I will break something."

Our eyes meet, and I realize he honestly didn't know his advance wasn't wanted. I feel bad for him, really. But he should have made sure. Although, yes, I should have been faster in telling him not to. "I'm sorry," he says.

I rush around him and Michaela, who is looking in the direction Seth went like she might go after him.

I run down the corridor, turn at the end, and nearly smack into Seth as he stands staring into the great room.

"I don't know where I'm going," he says.

"Music room?" I suggest.

"That... seems plausible." His head turns in the appropriate direction. "But I don't know if I can."

I frown, not following this conversation. If I'd had time to think about what we'd say to each other when I caught up to him, I'm certain it wouldn't have been this. "What do you mean?"

He looks at me over his shoulder, those blue eyes of his both watery and sharp. "I don't know if I can just walk away from you."

"Then don't."

His eyes lock onto mine as his body turns to face mine, the movement's grace not quite masking his pain. "You don't want me to?"

I shake my head and grab his hands. "No. Not even slightly."

He swallows, clearly wanting to believe me but afraid to. His eyes squeeze shut as his breath draws in. "You didn't stop him."

Swallowing an urge to whimper, I take comfort in the fact his hands have grasped mine back. "I swear I was about to. And I was trying to tell him I just want to be friends when he started. Did you hear any of that?"

"I heard you say his name," he admits. He slides his eyes open, ever so slowly. "It was really just him?"

I nod. "And I've already told him that if he tries again, I'm breaking bones."

The sides of his mouth curve up just a hair. "There might be a line."

"There may be," I agree. "But I'll be first in it. Proximity, you see."

His smile widens as he studies my face. Then it falters a little. "I..."

As he flounders for what he wants to say, I draw nearer, keeping his gaze trapped on mine. Slowly, giving him time to move away if he wants, I lift myself up on my toes and bring my lips to his. He sighs against them and his arms wrap around me. Like before, I feel his touch in every cell of my body. Kissing Seth may well be the most dangerous thing I've ever done; I could drown in him, and I wouldn't care.

He withdraws slowly, his hand coming up to stroke my hair. "I may be addicted to you. Would that be a problem?"

"Not for me. I like my boyfriends addicted." I smile before he leans down to kiss me again and I lose all sense of the rest of the world.

Chapter Twenty-Seven

Troy frowns as Seth and I come back into the room, and I can almost see the pieces clicking together in his brain. In Seth's place, most of the males I know would put an arm around me to make sure the message gets through, but Seth doesn't. From the way he kissed me, the problem isn't that he doesn't care, so I add a lack of possessiveness to his list of positive traits.

We settle on the couch, next to each other but with space between us. Michaela opens her mouth like she's about to speak, but then closes it again as a stoney faced Warren Denali storms into the room. He stops before her, crosses his arms, and glares in such a way as to make me very grateful that I'm not the one he's upset with.

Michaela tilts her head to the side and makes a little whimpering sound.

Warren glares a moment more, then melts and wraps his arms around his mate. His lips move in a whisper, probably telling her to never, ever do anything like that again. She nods against his chest and hugs him back, then they stand there looking perfect together.

My eyes go to Troy to see how he's handling this, and find him staring out the window with his back to the rest of us.

Seth's hand brushes my hair, drawing my attention to him. He smiles faintly and gestures toward Troy, silently telling me I should go talk to my friend. Fondness squeezes tight around my heart as I smile back in acknowledgement. I reach out to give his hand a squeeze before getting up and crossing the room.

As I draw up behind him, Troy glances over his shoulder. He watches quietly as I climb into the chair, twisted to face him. Now that I'm over here, I have no idea what to say.

"I'm going for a walk," Troy says, turning and stalking out the door.

I look to Seth, who shrugs, then follow Troy into the hallway. We walk for a few yards, then he spins to look at me. "Just tell me it's not because he's a snow leopard and I'm not."

So he's upset about me and Seth, not about Michaela and Warren. I'm not sure if I was hopeful for that or afraid of it. "No," I say softly, giving my head a shake to back the word up.

"No, it's not that, or no, you won't tell me?"

I sigh. "No, my feelings for Seth Dae are not based on his species."

Troy's eyes search mine.

"It only started this morning. That's why I hadn't told you."

He snorts. "It started well before this morning, kitten."

Guessing he's right, I nod. "But I was too blind to see it, so it doesn't count."

"It doesn't count?" He looks away, his shoulders slumping. "If that's true, then my only problem is being a few hours too late."

My memory provides me with an image of the night of the dance. If he had kissed me then… "No, I don't think that's the only problem."

"Is that supposed to make me feel better?" His head turns and his eyes come back to me. "Maybe you want to give me a complete list of my faults? Then I can see where I'm lacking."

I nearly tell him that his biggest flaw is his petulance, but I recognize he's only lashing out because he's in pain, so I tell him, "We'll talk later." And I leave him in the hallway.

Back in Becky's office, I text Penny, telling her that Troy could use a friend right now. Then I snuggle against Seth, and try not to feel guilty about how good it feels.

When Becky makes it back, Troy trails behind her with downcast eyes. My romantic drama fades into the background as I force myself to sit up straight and look at Becky.

I expect either a lecture or a tirade, but instead she sends us to our rooms to wait for Mr. Atherton's return.

When I hear the knock, I draw a ragged breath and prepare myself for facing the consequences of my actions. It's not someone summoning me to Mr. Atherton's office, though, but Amber.

She slides in quickly, shutting the door behind her. "Pretty sure you're not supposed to have guests," she explains.

"Then why are you here?"

She rolls her eyes. "Because I already sneaked into Seth's room."

"Oh." My eyes widen. "Oh."

"Indeed." She perches on the edge of my bed and cocks her head at me. "So you and my brother are a thing?"

My mouth flops about as I search for an answer. "Maybe? Did he say we are?"

Holding back a laugh, she nods. "As far as his mind is concerned, you are."

"And…" I swallow. "Does it bother you?"

"Because we were once paramores?" She shakes her head. "No, that bothers me not. As long as you treat him well, I am more than pleased to see you with my previously-hopeless sibling."

I let myself smile. "I'll try."

Her gaze latches onto mine. "Try harder than I did."

"What do you mean?"

She waits a breath to answer. "I mean, my darling friend, that I did not treat your heart with much gentleness."

"You didn't hurt me," I tell her.

Her eyebrow goes up.

"Okay, maybe a little," I admit. "But I never held it against you."

"So sayeth the nicest person in the world."

Another knock sounds on the door and Amber dashes into the bathroom.

This time it isn't a friend trying to sneak in. It's time to go see Mr. Atherton.

Chapter Twenty-Eight

The man behind the desk doesn't look threatening, but that does nothing to ease the knot in my stomach as I sit down across from my principal. None of the others are here, so I assume he's seeing us all separately. What I don't know is if that's good news or not.

He leans back in his chair as he watches me. There are circles under his eyes and unusual wrinkles around his mouth; but his blue sweater looks fresh, and his hair is clean. "So..." he says slowly. "You left the grounds when you weren't even allowed to leave the building. Whose idea was that?"

I swallow, bile rising in the back of my throat. "It was mine. I was worried about Troy and went looking for him. Michaela and Seth only followed along because they failed to stop me. They did try though. To stop me."

The tiniest of smiles teases Mr. Atherton's mouth, but he doesn't let it break out. "Oddly enough, I've asked three people that question and received three answers."

"Oh." My hands begin to tingle from poor circulation.

"I like that you're looking out for each other," Mr. Atherton says. "But I'd like to know the truth."

My lips press together, and my head bows down.

When I don't say anything, Mr. Atherton goes on. "Of course, I'd also like a billion dollars, and I don't think I'm getting that either."

I squint upwards. "Sir?"

He sighs, looking older all of a sudden. "There are people out there hunting my students. I can't have people thinking they can just disobey orders that were given for their safety."

"No, sir," I whisper.

"What would you do in my position?"

My shoulders shake as I draw a breath. "Expel me. But not the others. It was my idea."

"I know it wasn't your idea, Rina."

I bite my lip and make no reply.

"Everyone is on lockdown until the other yagers are found. You, however, are restricted to the building for a month following that. If you leave the building again, you will be expelled."

There are tears in my eyes as I nod. "And the others?"

"Same deal."

Relief rushes over me, and I realize I was more worried about them than myself. "Even Troy?"

Mr. Atherton's chair creaks as he shifts in it. "I haven't decided about him yet."

"You can't kick him out!" I stare earnestly at Mr. Atherton's eyes. "He doesn't have anywhere to go."

"I've been in contact with his parents," Mr. Atherton confides. "They are not as uncaring as he may have told you. I'm certain they would welcome him home. And... there are possibilities with the fae. He may be better off with them, as it appears he's not truly a were."

"The fae..." That would actually make sense. But the idea makes me sad. "He's been rejected so much already, sir. Please don't kick him out. If he wants to go, that's one thing, but please don't make him."

Our eyes lock for a few heartbeats before Mr. Atherton nods. "I'll certainly take that into consideration, Rina."

Sensing that's as good as I'm going to get, I ask to be excused and slip out the door.

In the hallway, Troy waits for his turn, Becky beside him. They walk into Mr. Atherton's office as soon as I get through the doorway. Neither of them say anything, and Troy doesn't look at me. Nevertheless, I lean against the wall and stare at the door as I wish I could hear through it. In a human school, I probably could, but this door was designed to keep nosey weres from eavesdropping.

The next thirty minutes drag out slowly and some time during them, I slide down the wall and fold my legs into a seated position. Sliding into a meditative state isn't as hard as I expected it to be, and I spend the time being aware of myself.

When the door finally opens, I'm feeling very grounded and ready to face Troy. If he's willing to face me.

Becky stops when she sees me. She gives me a faint smile, but goes into her own office without saying anything.

Troy folds his arms and looks down at me.

Now that he's here, I'm not sure what to say. Maybe I should have spent the last half hour thinking about that, huh? I swallow and try to smile. "Hey. So, I have a month's restriction and I'm on probation. You?"

"Same," he grunts. And he stares at me, like he's trying to see my soul. It makes me feel squirmy, and I channel that into motion to stand up.

"So you're staying?" I confirm.

His eyes still scorch into me. "Yeah. For now anyway."

I nod. "Good."

"Is it?"

A deep breath does little to settle my now-jangly nerves. I don't think I've gone from zenful to anxious quite this fast before. "Troy..."

"Yeah, yeah." He backs up, thumping against the wall between office doorways. "We're friends. I got the memo."

"Well, you're not acting like it," I hear myself point out.

His gaze drops to his shoes and he watches them for a few moments while I watch him. "You're right," he says eventually. He looks up. "I'm sorry. I'll do better."

"Alright."

His lips curl like they're smiling, but the rest of his face doesn't match up.

"I really am glad you're staying," I tell him.

"Yeah... thanks."

We stand silently, not looking at each other as we try to think of what to say.

"And thanks for rescuing me," he says after too long.

"It was mostly Michaela," I claim, looking up without moving my head.

He meets my eyes. "You didn't have to go with her. And she got captured; you didn't."

I shrug.

"Anyway..." He sighs loudly. "I'm going back to the library. Apparently I have to research faeries now."

A small laugh is all I can manage, but it's something.

We walk toward the library together, but when we get to its hallway, I hear the unmistakable sound of Seth playing piano, and I tell Troy goodbye so that I can drift over to the music room.

It's the same song Seth's been working on, I think, but it's a new part that I haven't heard before. It's both optimistic and nervous.

I wait for him to stop and start jotting down notes before I make noise to let him know I'm here. His head turns slowly and a shy sort of smile takes over his face.

"Hey," he says.

"Hey." I walk closer, smiling back.

"It's still not done." He gestures at his notebook with his pencil. "But it's getting there."

"Good."

I sit beside him on the bench, facing so that my back is to the piano, and we twist to face each other. As those gorgeous blue eyes of his devour me, I find myself hoping they never do shift to brown.

"Can I tell you a secret?" he asks, somewhere between serious and playful.

"Sure." My gaze tracks the notebook as he holds it up.

He flips back a few pages, going slowly as I watch and wonder if I'm supposed to be absorbing the music somehow. Then he gets to a page that's blank save for a title.

"Rina's Song?" I whisper. "This... This is my song? You've been writing me a song?"

His finger runs gently across the paper, underlining the words, and he smiles softly. "I knew it was yours from the beginning. I just didn't realize why I needed to be writing it."

Trembles take over my limbs. "When did you start it?"

"Around New Year's."

"New Year's?" That's a lot earlier than I would have guessed.

"Yeah." He closes the book, moving it aside before placing his palm against my cheek. His eyes flit away, but come back quickly. "You had champagne."

"Only one glass!"

A smile flickers across his face. "Apparently one glass is enough for you. You started singing in Russian. It sounded like a lullaby, but I had no idea what the words were."

Tears start to sting my eyes as I nod. "It was a song my grandmother used to sing to me when I was little."

"You sing it every year, but this year you seemed so much more lonely than before. Since we were kids, anyway."

My sniffle isn't the most attractive sound I've ever made. "Baba died two years after I got to Alaska. On New Year's." As I remember the response to my singing, the tears begin to fall in earnest. "Simone told me I sounded like a crow."

Solemn, he nods. "You sounded like an angel. But when she said that? That's when I knew I was going to have to Challenge."

I stare at the admission. "You... but I thought you Challenged because of Michaela."

"No." His second hand joins his first, so that my face is held in place. His thumbs rub against my tears. "She helped me find the strength to actually do it, but she didn't give me the idea. You can ask my parents. I talked to them about it before coming back from break."

"I believe you," I whisper. "I'm just not certain what the implications are."

His hands drop and find mine, grasping them tight. "The implications are that this is not a passing fancy." His gaze drops to my shoulder. "At the risk of scaring you off, I plan to be with you for as long as you'll let me. I don't want you to ever sound that lonely again. It nearly broke my heart before, but I think it might kill me now."

I lean back a little, focusing on the hair that runs alongside his cheekbone. "You really wouldn't have Challenged if you'd known the treaty was talking about me earlier, would you?"

He takes a long breath and presses his lips together before shaking his head. "No. I wouldn't have."

My heart breaks a little.

"But it's okay," he says quickly, bringing his eyes to mine. "You're right that it's better this way. I don't want you chained to me. I want you to choose to be with me."

I nod.

"Um… And you do, right?" he asks, so quietly it's hard to hear. "Choose to be with me?"

My lips twitch. I take just enough time to say, "Of course," before I silence us both with a kiss that's worth its own song.

Author's Note

When Rina says that her "wild cousins" aren't exactly plentiful, she's not exaggerating. Snow leopards, found in the mountains of central Asia, are increasingly rare. There may be fewer than four thousand of them in the wild, and they face many challenges, including habitat loss, lack of prey, poaching, and retaliatory killings by herders. They are not known to be aggressive toward humans, but too many humans are aggressive toward them.

To learn more about snow leopards, please visit the Snow Leopard Trust at snowleopard.org. They have a variety of educational resources, including a host of amazing photographs and videos, as well as a delightful shop selling hand-crafted merchandise from the snow leopards' lands.

www.ingramcontent.com/pod-product-compliance
Lightning Source LLC
Chambersburg PA
CBHW070818120626
46556CB00002B/553